PRAISE FOI

What newspapers say

"She keeps company with the best mystery writers" – *The Times*

"LJ Ross is the queen of Kindle" – *Sunday Telegraph*

"Holy Island is a blockbuster" – *Daily Express*

"A literary phenomenon" – *Evening Chronicle*

"A pacey, enthralling read" – *Independent*

What readers say

"I couldn't put it down. I think the full series will cause a divorce, but it will be worth it."

"I gave this book 5 stars because there's no option for 100."

"Thank you, LJ Ross, for the best two hours of my life."

"This book has more twists than a demented corkscrew."

"Another masterpiece in the series. The DCI Ryan mysteries are superb, with very realistic characters and wonderful plots. They are a joy to read!"

THE HAVEN

A SUMMER SUSPENSE MYSTERY

BOOKS BY LJ ROSS

THE ALEXANDER GREGORY THRILLERS:

1. *Impostor*
2. *Hysteria*
3. *Bedlam*
4. *Mania*
5. *Panic*

THE DCI RYAN MYSTERIES:

1. *Holy Island*
2. *Sycamore Gap*
3. *Heavenfield*
4. *Angel*
5. *High Force*
6. *Cragside*
7. *Dark Skies*
8. *Seven Bridges*
9. *The Hermitage*
10. *Longstone*
11. *The Infirmary (Prequel)*
12. *The Moor*
13. *Penshaw*
14. *Borderlands*
15. *Ryan's Christmas*
16. *The Shrine*
17. *Cuthbert's Way*
18. *The Rock*
19. *Bamburgh*
20. *Lady's Well*
21. *Death Rocks*

THE SUMMER SUSPENSE MYSTERIES:

1. *The Cove*
2. *The Creek*
3. *The Bay*
4. *The Haven*

THE HAVEN

A SUMMER SUSPENSE MYSTERY

LJ ROSS

ISBN: 978-1-912310-94-4

First published in August 2024 by Dark Skies Publishing

Author photo by Gareth Iwan Jones

Cover artwork by Andrew Davidson

Typesetting and cover layout by
Riverside Publishing Solutions

Printed and bound by CPI Goup (UK) Limited

CHAPTER 1

Wednesday evening

Central Television Studios, Dublin

Isolde Malone blinked several times, but there was no denying the truth.

She couldn't read the auto-cue.

The words swam in front of her eyes, nothing but a jumble of white letters against a black screen. It wasn't the first time it had happened lately and yet, according to the best optometrist in the city, she had perfect vision and shouldn't have any trouble reading at a distance, let alone the couple of metres separating her newsreader's desk and the little black box that displayed her script.

Probably stress, her doctor told her. *Try to take it easy.*

If the programme hadn't been live, broadcasting to all of her native Ireland, then she might have laughed there and then at the thought of it. Until the past couple of months, she'd have described herself as the type of person who *thrived* on stressful scenarios, and she'd certainly never suffered any blurred vision as a consequence. It had taken years of drive and determination to climb the slippery ladder of success, but she'd done it and could now be proud of a career and lifestyle that was the envy of her peers. Isolde was the *face* of Irish television, with lucrative sponsorship and advertising deals on the side, a smart townhouse overlooking the River Liffey and a string of handsome men ready and waiting at the drop of a hat, if she wanted them. It was a good life, doing the work she loved, and she was grateful for it.

Yet all of that couldn't help her to read the screen, and precious seconds ticked by as the air fell dead.

Isolde? Wake up!

Go to the weather!

Owen, the show's producer, almost shouted through her earpiece and she came to attention, pasting a bright smile on her face.

"Ah—well now, I think it's time we found out what to expect of the weather this weekend. What can you tell us, Maeve?"

Her colleague and, as it happened, her friend and housemate, picked up the prompt seamlessly.

"Thanks Isolde, well, I can tell you that it's very good news for anybody hoping to get out and about this weekend, with clear blue skies expected from Saturday right through until Sunday lunchtime—"

Afforded a moment's respite, Isolde kept a smile on her face, mentally rehearsing the outro she planned to say, and was ready by the time the camera came back to her.

"Thank you, Maeve! We'll all have to remember our sunscreen, won't we?" She paused to smile at her friend, who knew the routine and said something about viewers remembering to stay hydrated. Then, Isolde smiled beautifully for the viewers at home. "Well, that's about it from us here at Channel One News; we'll see you bright and early for the morning news at six tomorrow. Until then, a very good evening to all of you."

She shuffled a sheaf of papers as the end credits played, her face composed into professional lines.

Breathe, she thought. *Just keep breathing.*

Three...two...one...clear!

As soon as they were off-air, she slumped forward against the desk, holding her head in her hands. Maeve hurried across the studio to slip an arm around her shoulders, concern writ large across her lovely face.

"Isolde! What's the matter? Can I get you anything—a glass of water? Ah, hell with that, a glass of *gin*?"

Isolde raised watery eyes to smile at her friend. "No, I'll—I'll be all right, I just—"

"What *happened* back there?"

Owen O'Grady rushed to join them and, though his bedside manner might have left something to be desired, she knew there was concern behind the brusque enquiry—for her, and for the show he was tasked to produce.

"I'm so sorry, Owen," she muttered. "I know this is the fourth time it's happened in the past couple of weeks...I don't know what to say. My vision just suddenly…" She swallowed sudden, unexpected tears, and made a helpless motion with her hands. "It just *went*. I couldn't read anything on the auto-cue, and I panicked."

Sympathy flickered in his eyes. "Have you seen an optician about it?"

She nodded, miserably. "A doctor, as well. Neither of them can find anything wrong with me," she said. "I'm exhausted all the time and I've not been sleeping too well, so they reckon it's just stress. I've got another appointment with the doctor to talk about having a scan or some blood tests, in case…in case there's something wrong with my brain. Apparently, if you have a tumour, it can affect your vision sometimes."

Even saying the words aloud caused her stomach to perform a slow somersault.

"I'm sure it's *nothing* like that," Maeve said quickly, and gave her a reassuring squeeze. "There's probably all kinds of reasons why you're having problems with your sight, as well as the headaches and all that. Isn't that right, Owen?"

He was a bit slow on the uptake, but got there in the end. "Aye—that's right," he intoned. "It's probably nothing at all to worry about."

Isolde looked between them, at their forced smiles, and felt even worse than before.

Owen reached across and took both of her hands, already hating himself for the decision he had to make. "Look, Isolde, I think... You know, with things being as they are..." He cleared his throat, awkwardly. "It might be best if you took a little bit of time off. A sabbatical—"

She opened her mouth to protest, but he overrode any objection.

"Just long enough for you to get to the bottom of things and feel better, that's all. We all love you here, you know that. The public love you too—don't they, Maeve?" Her friend nodded, vigorously. "You've got the best viewing figures in the whole of Ireland and the show's ratings have never been higher," he continued. "We'll all be waiting here for you when you come back, so don't worry about that."

Isolde wanted to believe he was right, and that she'd have a job to come back to after a short sabbatical, but she knew as well as they did that the public could be a fickle bunch and so could the management team at Channel One.

She also knew that he wasn't giving her a choice.

Summoning whatever was left of her pride, she gave him one of her trademark smiles and affected an air of blithe nonchalance.

"That's a grand idea," she said. "I'll take a few days away and be fit as a fiddle in no time."

"That's the spirit!" Owen patted her hand in a manner she found vaguely condescending.

"Do you want me to come home with you, now?" Maeve offered. "Just to make sure you're all right?"

Isolde smiled again at her friend. "Ah, no, I couldn't ask it," she said. "I know you've got a date with Rob after work tonight, and we can't have you missing that."

"I don't mind, really—"

Isolde shook her head. "Honestly, the pair of you are clucking around me like hens," she said lightly. "I probably just need a good nights' sleep and a bubble bath. I'll be back on the horse by the end of the week."

"All the same, let me organise a taxi to take you home," Owen said, clearly unconvinced by her performance.

Since a dull, throbbing headache was making its way across her optic nerve, Isolde didn't bother to argue the point. "Thanks," she said softly.

With a heavy heart, she took one last, lingering look at her desk and then made her way back to her dressing room to collect her things.

CHAPTER 2

An hour later, Isolde stepped inside the little house she owned on an exclusive part of Dublin's waterfront. It was a vibrant part of town, thriving with families and young professionals, and usually she loved the buzz of it all. She liked that the coffee vendor at the end of the street knew her favourite tipple, that the newsagent always asked after her family despite never having met them, and that she never felt alone amid the hustle and bustle of the city. She and Maeve were both attractive young women who enjoyed life and shared its ups and downs together, laughing over a glass of wine or a takeaway in front of the telly, and the situation suited them both perfectly. Now, as Isolde toed out of the smart heels she'd worn for work, she found she was lonely in the surrounding quiet and wished she'd accepted her friend's offer of company, after all.

Shrugging it off, she padded through to the kitchen, her footsteps silent against the polished wooden floor as she went in search of something to tempt her ailing stomach. The fridge was full of her usual favourites, but, after a cursory inspection, she let the door swing shut again and held a hand to her abdomen as it protested the very sight of food.

"What's the *matter* with me?" she whispered to the empty space.

There was no reply and Isolde felt a keening pain in her chest that, for once, had nothing to do with her mystery ailment, and everything to do with missing family.

Rhona and Gerald Malone had been divorced long ago, while she and her brother were still teenagers, and she supposed they were all the happier for it. She could still remember their raging arguments and the harsh insults they'd thrown at one another, while she and Luke had sought to drown out their voices with cartoons, or else leave the house in search of happier climes. Nowadays, their parents lived separate lives, her father having taken himself off for a quiet life in the country, surrounded by acres of land and the occasional company of a neighbouring widow who stayed over from time to time and didn't mind talking about golf or football fixtures. Meanwhile, her mother had gone off in search of adventure on the Gold Coast of Australia, where she'd promptly met a man with a year-round tan and a lust for life to satisfy her own. Even her brother, Luke, had emigrated to England, of all places, and made a happy life for himself on the Cornish coast with his new wife, Gabrielle. She was glad they'd found the people and places that made them happy; she only wished they lived around the corner, especially now.

As if to reinforce her feelings, another stabbing pain ricocheted through her stomach, so strong she was forced to lean back against the counter to catch her breath. Once the pain subsided, she scrubbed weak tears from her eyes, then reached for the kettle.

"A cup of herbal tea," she muttered. "A bit of chocolate and a bath while I watch *Pride and Prejudice*. That'll do the trick."

Fifteen minutes later, she dragged her weary feet upstairs and balanced a small tray on a table beside the bath. Her muscles relaxed instantly as they hit the fragrant water, and she levered herself up to take a sip of tea, choosing to ignore the persistent shake to her hands and the feeling of acute tiredness that seemed to be her daily companion. She angled her smartphone against the teapot and settled back to enjoy one of her favourite period dramas from the 1990s, something she was sure would never fit with her current 'image' on television but which, she was also sure, she had absolutely no intention of changing.

There were few ailments that couldn't be cured with a good dose of Colin Firth, after all.

Shortly after Elizabeth Bennet was first introduced to the scoundrel George Wickham, Isolde's eyelids succumbed to fatigue and began to droop. She listened to the familiar voices playing on the miniature screen, allowing her limbs to float as the pains and frustrations of the day were overtaken briefly by the comforting nostalgia of one of life's little pleasures.

Then, she heard it.

A footstep, on the wooden floor downstairs.

Her eyes flew open, and she gripped the edge of the bath with slippery fingers, moving carefully into a seated position as she waited, her senses on high alert. After a moment, she began to think she'd imagined it, and that her mind was playing tricks at the end of a long day.

She froze, as the sound came again.

This time, a creak on the stairs.

Fighting the urge to hurry and thereby draw attention to her whereabouts, she stopped the programme and dragged herself up and out of the bath as quietly as she could. Grasping a towel, she wrapped it around her shivering body and cast around for a weapon with wide, frightened eyes. There was only an electric toothbrush and the teapot, but there was no time to grab either implement before the soft but distinct sound of approaching footsteps reached the landing outside. Fear stole the breath from her body and her eye fell on the door, which she'd closed out of habit but not bothered to lock. Galvanised, she dashed across the room to slide the bathroom lock into place, wincing as the sound seemed to echo around the tiled walls.

Seconds later, she heard the footsteps come to a standstill outside, and she clasped a hand against her own mouth, willing herself to stay upright as her mind raced.

Had one of those sad, lonely men who sent disturbing fan mail found out where she lived?

Her first thought was to find a means of escape, but there was only a small, high window in the bathroom, and she knew it would be a futile endeavour to try to get out that way, which left only one option.

If it came to it, she would have to fight.

Endless seconds ticked by as she stood there, plastered against the wall to the side of the doorway, while another person stood on the other side of it. She felt their presence, and, to her feverish mind, it seemed that she and the stranger were locked in a battle of wills, both waiting for the other to make the first move.

Then, the stalemate was broken.

In horror, she watched as the door handle began to turn this way and that, moving slowly at first, and then with more vigour, rattling against the doorframe as they tried to force it open.

Almost blinded by panic, Isolde snatched up her phone to call the police. Her fingers were clumsy against the screen and a sob escaped her lips as she dropped it on the tiles at her feet. She scrambled to retrieve it as the intruder began kicking the bathroom door, working hard to break it from its hinges as she stood there, naked and vulnerable, with nowhere to run.

She keyed in the digits but before she could hear the first comforting words from a police operator, the door gave way, splintering open to reveal a figure dressed entirely in black. Their face was covered by a ski mask, but their eyes locked with hers and she knew she would never forget the nightmarish silhouette so long as she lived.

If she lived to remember it, at all.

She opened her mouth to scream, the sound ending on a strangled gasp as the figure stepped inside, advancing towards her with slow, purposeful steps. She shrank away in reflex, the action causing her to slip on the wet floor underfoot, and then she was falling, down and down until her head met the hard marble floor with a *crack*.

The last thing she remembered was the shadow looming above her, a spectre without a name or a face.

CHAPTER 3

Isolde awoke cold and shivering on the floor, her towel having dislodged itself so that it hung in a damp knot around her waist. She began to struggle upward, which caused an immediate tidal wave of pain to pound mercilessly against the right side of her head. Raising a tentative hand to her skull, she found a small area of matted blood that was still wet to the touch and, suddenly, everything came rushing back.

The intruder, coming towards her, dressed in black.

Their eyes, just as dark…

She had been completely prone, unable to defend herself against an attack, nor even to remember it, as she'd been knocked out by the fall. Battling tears, she made a quick inspection and was pleased to find no obvious signs of physical trauma other than the head injury, but that was something she'd need to have checked out by a medical professional to be completely sure.

Irrational shame swept over her then, and she allowed herself a few ragged tears before thrusting the feeling aside, telling herself she'd deal with the trauma of her encounter another day.

Then, with slow, careful movements, she raised herself up again and listened for any sound that might tell her the intruder was still in the house.

Silence.

Her phone had fallen from her hand and, after a tense moment in which she feared it had been stolen, she located it behind a basket of towels and hurriedly keyed in the number for the Dublin police. Still fearful that the intruder would come back, she hid herself behind the door and whispered replies to the operator who answered her call. After it was done, and she was left with a promise that someone would be with her in a matter of minutes, Isolde decided to take their advice and contact a friend.

Maeve answered after the third ring, and she heard the rumble of a busy restaurant in the background.

"Isolde? Is everything alright?"

Relief coursed through her system, making her tearful all over again. "Maeve, I—*no*, no, I'm not alright. There was a—an intruder..." She paused, drawing herself in, bearing down against the shock that was causing her body to shake uncontrollably. "They broke into the house and then forced their way into the bathroom, where I'd—I'd been in the bath—"

"Oh my God," Maeve breathed, and then said something to her dinner date about getting the bill immediately. "I'm so sorry, love. Have they—I mean—are you hurt...like *that*?"

Isolde swallowed bile. "No—at least, I don't think so. I've hurt my head, though. I fell on the tiles in the bathroom and hit it pretty hard. I was trying—I was trying to get away, but there was nowhere to go." A small sound escaped her throat, an echo of the terror she'd felt.

"I'm on my way home now," Maeve told her firmly, in the kind of no-nonsense tone she needed to hear. "I've left Rob to sort out the bill, and I'm going to hail a cab. I'll be back in ten minutes—or even less if it's Mad Andy who's doing the driving."

Isolde tried to work up a smile as she thought of the local taxi driver they'd dubbed 'Mad Andy', on account of his persistent and flagrant abuse of the Rules of the Road.

"Thanks," she managed. "Hurry, please."

Maeve arrived home in record time thanks to the aforementioned Andy's best efforts, and found Isolde sitting in the living room wrapped in a fluffy dressing gown, cup of tea in hand while a paramedic tended to the wound on her head and a police officer from the local Garda Station made a note of her statement.

"Isolde!" Maeve rushed into the room, swept past both emergency service officers, and plonked herself on the sofa so that she could envelop her friend in an enormous hug.

"*Maeve*. Oh, God, I'm so pleased to see you."

"I can't believe what's happened," her friend mumbled, still holding her tight in a bear-like embrace.

Then, she turned to the others.

"How *did* this happen?" she demanded. "This is a nice part of town. What's the place coming to, if a woman can't even take a bath in her own home without being attacked—"

"I wasn't physically attacked, that I know of," Isolde said, dully.

"You'd never have fallen, if whoever it was hadn't frightened you," Maeve said, and then pinned the police officer with a stare. "Well? What're you going to do about it?"

The officer, who was already starstruck at the sight of one of the country's most recognisable faces, was doubly struck by the presence of her weather girl, too.

He puffed out his chest a bit. "We've already found out how they managed to gain entry into the property," he told them, and waited for the inevitable praise.

When it was not forthcoming, his chest deflated again.

"Through the back door," he said. "Not very original, but it's the best way to get inside, given the location of the house. The door backs straight on to the waterway, where you can pick up the cycle and pedestrian route along the river. It's an easy job for an experienced thief to jimmy the lock and let themselves in without causing much of a stir, or even make a passer-by look twice."

"The alarm—" Maeve began.

"Wasn't on, because I was in the house and thought it wasn't necessary," Isolde whispered.

Maeve took her hand, and squeezed. "Don't blame yourself for this."

Isolde nodded, but began folding and refolding the edge of her dressing gown, closing her eyes briefly as the paramedic finished bandaging the wound at her head.

"Not as bad as it looks," the woman pronounced. "There's some swelling, and I think you should come along to the hospital for observation this evening so that we can watch out for any concussion."

Isolde thought about mentioning the existing problems she'd been having, then thought better of it, unwilling to waste their valuable time on things that probably had no bearing on the matters at hand.

"Is there anything we can do to help?" Maeve asked the police officer.

He blew out a tired breath. "You could have a look around and see if anything's missing," he said. "Since your friend wasn't assaulted as far as we know, we should explore the possibility that this was a straightforward burglary attempt. As you said yourself, Miss, this is a nice area, so there'll always be thieves on the lookout for an easy smash and grab."

Isolde frowned. "That can't be right," she said. "If he'd wanted to steal our valuables, he could have gone straight into the bedrooms and raided for jewellery, or made for the study to try to find documents for identity theft or whatever. Why would he bother to intimidate me behind a locked bathroom door, if it wasn't to—to—you know."

Maeve nodded. "I agree," she said, and gave her hand another squeeze. "You're sure it was a man, then?"

The officer looked up at that, and made a swift note to himself to remember to include the question earlier in the statement he was recording, lest anyone should think he'd forgotten to ask it himself.

Isolde thought back, recalling the figure to her mind, and then nodded slowly.

"Everything about them seemed male," she said eventually. "The height—maybe six feet, or a bit over—and they were muscular, from what I could tell. It all seemed to happen so quickly, I can't be sure..."

Her mind had already forgotten some of the details her eyes might have seen, which was part of the body's natural defence when dealing with traumatic events.

"Don't worry too much," the officer said. "More details might come back to you over the next few days, and you can contact us at any time."

Isolde nodded, and took the small white card he offered. "I'll give you all I can," she said, and felt more tired than she could ever remember feeling in her entire life. "The mask, the clothes, they were all decent quality black ski gear...oh, whoever it was wore ski gloves, too. There was a bit of skin visible around their eyes and it looked white Caucasian, to me."

The officer nodded, and added it to the description. "What about the eyes?" he asked. "Do you remember what colour they were?"

"I wasn't close enough to notice the exact colour...I only remember that they seemed very *dark*, but I don't know whether my memory has been clouded..."

She clasped her fingers around the mug of tea she still held, and took a sip of the lukewarm liquid to give herself something to do.

"That's surely enough for now," Maeve said, eyeing the officer again. "You're almost fit to drop and we need to get you to the hospital. I'll go and have a look around our bedrooms and see if there's anything missing, then we'll make a plan—"

"Be careful not to touch any surfaces," the officer said. "Forensics will be on their way."

A couple of minutes later, Maeve returned.

"I can't find anything missing," she said. "Nothing obvious, anyhow. Does that mean it wasn't a thief, after all? What if it was someone who came here to hurt Isolde, or scare her in some way?" She didn't wait for a reply, but put a comforting hand around her friend's shoulder. "I don't think it's safe for either of us to stay here, in the circumstances."

The officer nodded. "I'd certainly recommend you stay somewhere else tonight, once your friend has been checked over at the hospital. Do you have family nearby?"

Maeve did, but she knew it was a sore point for Isolde, whose family was scattered around the world. All the same, after the fright she'd had, on top of the sabbatical she was forced to take, it seemed like a good idea to spend some quality time around those who loved her even more than the Irish viewing public.

"What about going to visit Luke and Gabrielle?" she suggested. "They sent you that invitation the other week—you know? For a fancy weekend at that lovely hotel. It might be just what you need!"

Isolde thought of her brother and his wife, then of the gilded invitation that had arrived in the post around a month ago inviting her to a special charity auction to be held at the Tintagel Hotel. In addition to being a celebrated artist in his own right, her brother owned a string of art galleries. The idea was that all of the glitterati of Cornwall and the neighbouring counties would turn out for a weekend of networking and socialising, designed to encourage them to dip into their deep pockets and bid for all manner of interesting artefacts and experiences, and artwork provided by Luke, the proceeds of which would go to a number of worthy causes in the local area. The hotel itself had been completely refurbished, and Luke's event was designed to coincide with its grand opening, or so he'd told her.

A quick calculation of the dates reminded her that the event was only a few days away.

"I don't know," she murmured. "They're probably not expecting me, and it's short notice. Besides, they'll be busy organising the weekend auction, anyway—"

"Don't be silly," Maeve told her, in no uncertain terms. "Luke will be delighted to see you, and it'll do you the world of good to get away from it all for a while. Why not spend your sabbatical over there and enjoy some of the Cornish beaches rather than stewing here in the city?"

Isolde was torn. On the one hand, leaving Ireland for Cornwall took her further away from the life she had built, and further away from the minds of the television producers who employed her.

On the other hand, she missed her brother terribly, and couldn't stand to stay in her own home for another night.

She came to a decision. "I'll call him, first thing in the morning."

Maeve smiled. "You never know," she said, wickedly. "You might find a *Tristan*, while you're in the area."

Isolde snorted. "I've never met one I liked yet."

"There's a first time for everything," her friend quipped. "Imagine the story you could tell your grandchildren."

Isolde rolled her eyes, and thought privately that the events of the evening had obviously addled her friend's brain even more than they had her own. Her parents had named her for the heroine in the old Celtic legend of Tristan and Iseult, a tragic tale of the illicit love between a Cornish knight and an Irish princess in the days of King Arthur. Their story didn't have a happy ending, she recalled, just as her parent's hadn't, either. It was hardly surprising, then, that she harboured few romantic notions about love and marriage, and words like 'forever'.

She'd never believed in fairy tales, and wasn't about to start now.

CHAPTER 4

Friday morning

Isolde gripped the edge of her seat in the tiny propellor plane as it continued its choppy descent towards Newquay Airport and wondered, idly, what music they would play at her funeral. As the wings dipped perilously back and forth, in perfect tandem with her stomach, she could only be sorry that she hadn't found the time to wish her friends and family a more meaningful farewell before stepping aboard the glorified tin can.

"Ladies and gents, this is your captain speaking," a mellow, West Country voice announced. "We've got a bit of headwind on our approach into

Newquay, so it might be a bit of a bumpy landing, but it's nothing to worry about. Hold on to your arses, and we'll be there dreckly."

Dreckly? When a Cornishman told you something was about to happen 'dreckly', it meant anything but 'directly'. In fact, it was far more likely they'd be landing sometime in the middle of next week.

They proceeded to circle the runway three times.

"Our Father, who art in Heaven..." she muttered to herself.

The plane tipped to one side, and she squeezed her eyes shut, before prising them open again to see the dramatic cliffs and aqua-blue waters framed beautifully in the little window at her side. Any doubts she might have felt about her prospects of survival during the course of the next five to ten minutes were momentarily blotted out by the vista, and she understood then why Luke had fallen in love with the landscape.

After a hair-raising moment in which she and her fellow passengers made their peace with God and pacts with the Devil, the plane's wheels finally hit the tarmac with a skid, and a collective cheer rose up amongst the small crowd. Almost giddy with relief, Isolde disembarked the aircraft, shielding her eyes as she stepped out into a glorious summer's day. The airport itself was tiny, only a single terminal building, and she was relieved again to be met with a familiar face when she entered the arrivals hall.

"Luke!" She would have known him anywhere. Luke Malone stood out amongst a crowd, being tall, dark, and with similarly even, attractive features to her own. Seeing her brother there in the flesh transported her back in time, to when they were both young and would play together in the garden of their childhood home or fight over a game of Monopoly, before life had moved on, as it inevitably did.

His face broke into a wide grin and he dodged the other passengers with ease, moving forward to catch her up into a warm embrace.

"Hello, stranger," he said, and she smiled against the rough material of his wax jacket, holding on to him for a little longer than was necessary while she swallowed a rising tide of emotion.

Sensing it, he pulled away so that he could look at her properly.

"*Hey*," he said softly. "Is everything okay?"

Her lip wobbled, but she forced herself to smile brightly, just as she did for the cameras.

"Of course—" she started to say, but couldn't bring herself to lie. "Although…it's been a bit of a difficult time, lately."

Instantly concerned, not only by her words but by the pale, gaunt look of her, he reached for her bag with one hand and slipped the other around her shoulders.

"C'mon," he said. "Let's get out of here, and you can tell me what's been going on."

Feeling safe for the first time since her ordeal, Isolde allowed herself to lean on him and be led from the terminal building towards the car park.

As she clambered inside his battered Land Rover, she was met with another friendly face from the back seat.

"Madge!"

Luke's Golden Retriever was a truly unique animal, from her glossy coat to the elegant tilt of her head, which seemed appropriate given that she'd been named after a bona fide pop icon. Isolde spent a couple of minutes ruffling her fur, already feeling better than she had in days.

"I missed her," Isolde said, fondly.

Luke smiled. "She's been a busy girl, since you last visited," he said, and gave the dog a knowing look. "Madge is a mother now, to four adorable puppies."

Isolde beamed. "I didn't know you'd planned—"

"She didn't have any help or introductions from us," he said, with a chuckle. "It was all thanks to a wild night on the beach with a visiting Labrador, who swept her off her paws, apparently."

He sighed, and shook his head. "I have to say, it was tough to let them go," he said. "But they all went to excellent homes. Two of them are still in Carnance, just a couple of doors down from us, so Madge can visit whenever she likes. My friend, Nick, took the third for his family—you'll meet him and his wife, Kate, this weekend. They have a little boy who loves dogs and has been begging for one of his own, so it was perfect timing. As for the fourth, she's living the high life in St Ives with a shopkeeper friend of mine, Jacqui."

Isolde rubbed his arm. "You always did love animals," she said.

"They're often kinder than humans," he replied, with a wry smile.

She knew they were thinking of the same thing. Around the time they'd been caught in the crossfire of their parents' matrimonial breakdown, their old family dog, Spud, had been a therapeutic friend to both of them and having to say goodbye to that gentle creature had been the first major grief of their lives.

"What happened to your head?" he said, changing the subject. "It looks like you've had a bit of a tumble."

Isolde had decided to wait until they saw one another in person before telling him what had happened; partly, because she couldn't bring herself to talk about it anymore after hours spent dealing with the police and paramedics, and, partly, because she wanted to forget. However, she wasn't in the habit of keeping secrets, so she took a deep breath and gave him the headlines in clipped tones, as if she was delivering a news report—it was easier, that way.

Luke held her hand as she spoke, and, when she fell silent, drew her into his arms for another hard hug. "I'm sorry you went through that," he said, gruffly. "Have they found him?"

He started up the engine with a flick of his wrist, and she realised that he was angry.

Very angry.

She shook her head, and turned to watch the passing landscape as they made the journey from the airport to Tintagel, where they would be staying.

"The investigation is ongoing," she said, repeating the hackneyed words she'd been told by the police. "I know some of it was my fault. I should have had the alarm on, even when I was inside, I should have checked the camera at the back door—"

"For pity's sake, Isolde. Nobody puts the alarm on when they're in their own home unless they're locking up for the night," he said. "Even then, most people don't bother. You're entitled to feel safe within your own four walls, and you're not to blame for someone choosing to violate your space, or trying to violate you."

Isolde glanced at her brother, and thought that she'd never loved him more. "Thanks, Luke," she said. "I needed to hear that."

He nodded, obviously still reeling, and she hesitated about telling him about the other problems she'd been having.

"I suppose that's why you've taken a sabbatical," he said, half to himself. "It's a good idea to take some time away if you need it."

That decided the matter, she thought, and sucked in another deep breath to tell him the rest.

"Actually Luke, I'd already decided to take some time away," she said, keeping her eyes firmly on the fields as they whipped through country lanes that hugged the jagged coastline. "I haven't been feeling very well, lately."

He looked away from the road briefly to cast his eyes over her.

"Why didn't you tell me any of this on the phone?" he muttered. "I could have flown over to see you!"

"I know how busy you are—" she began.

"I'm *never* too busy for my family, Isolde," he said. "I'm always here for you, whenever you need me and even when you don't. Gabi is, too. In fact, she asked me to tell you she's sorry she couldn't make it to the airport but she's at some bookseller's lunch in Truro today, so she'll see you in time for dinner at the hotel this evening."

Isolde nodded, having been a big fan of her sister-in-law from their first encounter. "It'll be grand to see her," she said.

"But what's this about you not being well?" he persisted. "It must be bad, if you're taking time off."

Now it came to it, she felt foolish even talking about it. "I—oh, it's probably nothing at all," she said, breezily. "I had a few funny turns at work, where I couldn't read the auto-cue, and I've been faint and unwell with the occasional bad head and stomach-ache."

More than occasional, she added silently.

"But, you know, all of those things could be down to stress," she tagged on. "In fact, that's what the doctor seems to think it is."

Luke heard fear beneath the bravado, something his sister rarely showed.

"It's okay to feel scared," he told her. "You've always been so fit and healthy, Isolde. It must have come as a huge shock, especially since you say these incidents have been happening at work. I know how much you pride yourself on doing the best job you can."

She nodded, grateful that he understood her so well that it precluded any need to explain herself.

"I've been so frustrated," she admitted. "The worst thing is not knowing the cause. If only the doctor told me it was one thing or another to blame, at least I could take some tablets or…oh, I don't know what. I've been drinking all the herbal teas, taking the multi-vitamins, and eating so much spinach, I'd give Popeye a run for his money."

Luke indicated left to leave the B-road they'd been following and turned along another minor road which would take them to the village of Tintagel and, beyond it, to the hotel.

"Do you think the doctor is right about it all being to do with stress?" he asked.

She lifted a shoulder. "I guess everyone feels stressed, from time to time," she admitted. "But I love my work and I love my life. I wouldn't have thought any everyday stress I might feel was bad enough to cause all these symptoms."

Luke wasn't so sure, but he didn't press the point because he trusted his sister to be the best judge of her own mind. "Well," he said, and gave her a reassuring smile. "We'll just have to figure out what's the matter, won't we?"

"*We?*"

"That's right, *eejit*," he said, giving her a playful shove. "You might be a capable, independent woman, but you don't have to go through all of this alone."

Isolde looked at her big brother and struggled to find the words she wanted to say, so instead fell back on plain truth. "I love you, Luke."

"I love you, too," he said, and then added for good measure, "y' daft article."

CHAPTER 5

Tintagel was a picturesque village, situated only a stone's throw from a ruined mediaeval castle of the same name, which occupied a dramatic position atop a rugged clifftop peninsula on Cornwall's northern coastline. It was accessible from the mainland via a network of steep, narrow pathways or a high iron bridge, which allowed the many thousands of tourists who visited each year to trample around the old fortress which had, for many centuries, been reputed as the site of King Arthur's legendary Camelot. Some said it was the site of his conception, after the wizard, Merlin, used his sorcery to disguise King Uther Pendragon, Arthur's father, as Gorlois, the Duke of Cornwall, husband of Arthur's mother, Igraine.

Isolde remembered this portion of the old Arthurian legend as they crawled through the quaint streets and reflected that, even centuries ago, men were finding ways to be duplicitous with their women. She was not a misandrist; in fact, she had plenty of male friends and occasional relationships, but, if she was honest, had it not been for her brother, she might have thought that *all* men were not to be trusted, especially given her most recent experience.

How would you know? her mind whispered. *You've never given any of them a chance.*

"Tell me about the hotel," she said, as they drove through the village and followed a winding road towards the cliffs.

"It's a beautiful old manor house," he began by saying. "It's right on the clifftops overlooking the Celtic Sea to the north and the castle is just a few minutes' walk further to the west. You can see it from the bedroom windows."

"Sounds lovely," she admitted. "You said it was renovated recently?"

Luke nodded.

"For years, it was just a family home," he said. "The Williams' are an old family in these parts, and they happen to own a chain of luxury hotels around the world—"

"Wait a minute," she said. "You mean the Williams Hotel Group?"

"That's the one. Do you know it?"

Isolde had enjoyed many a spa day at The Celtic Grand in Dublin, which was part of that group of hotels, as well as the Ashlin Castle Hotel, another fabulous country pile in County Clare that now served as a retreat for over-stressed city workers such as herself.

"I've been to a couple," she said. "Lovely places, all of them. And the Tintagel Hotel is their family home? Why would they want to turn it into a hotel?"

Before he could answer, the building itself suddenly came into view, stately and dramatic; framed by a set of stone pillared gates at the end of a long, well-kept driveway, with only the sea and the sky as its backdrop.

"Wow," she breathed.

Luke chuckled, and made the turn through the gates. "Not too shabby, eh? Harry and Meg Williams lived here and used it as their base, when they weren't travelling around building up the hotel business," he said. "Sadly, Harry passed away a couple of years ago, and I think Meg felt a bit lonely rattling around the old place. She lives in a kind of dowager annex beside the main house and has signed over the business to her son, who's running the bulk of it now and spends most of his time overseas. His uncle, Mark, works in the business too and has been managing the hotel and the refurbishments ahead of its grand opening."

"A real family operation, then," she said, and Luke nodded.

"I came to know them through Meg," he said. "She's a patron of the arts and lifelong philanthropist. She and her husband became fabulously wealthy, but they haven't forgotten their roots or the local community here. It was her idea to offer us the hotel as a venue for the charity auction, all expenses paid, and her son's thrown in a few holidays at their hotels around the world as part of the auction offering."

"Good people," Isolde murmured.

"You can judge for yourself, when you meet them this evening," he said with a cheerful smile. "I've invited a few of our friends along for the weekend, too, so it won't be all business. There should be plenty of time for fun, with walks and relaxation in between."

She looked through the windshield as they came up to the entrance of the hotel, noted the weathered stone crenelations and trailing ivy, the mullioned windows and manicured lawns and, beyond all that, Tintagel Castle further along the cliffs to the west, looking every inch the mythical, ethereal place that had inspired so many artists and writers through the years.

Watching the play of emotions passing over his sister's face, Luke smiled.

"Welcome to Cornwall," he said softly.

They were shown into the hotel by an attentive concierge, who insisted upon taking her suitcase before ushering them inside a large, oak-panelled hallway resplendent with flowers, soft lighting and the happy chatter of other guests who'd gathered to socialise on some of the comfortable leather sofas arranged in the snug areas. It was warm and welcoming, as was the aforementioned Mark, who recognised Luke and raised a friendly hand before crossing the chequered tiles to greet them. He was a tall, lean man with a shock of silver-grey hair and tanned skin that spoke of days spent outdoors and on the beach, but he wore a smart, tailored suit and a tie bearing the Williams family crest, which featured on much of the hotel merchandise and stationery. He might have been sixty or thereabouts, but had the demeanour of a man at least ten years younger.

"Good to see you again, Luke! And this must be your lovely wife?"

Luke took his outstretched hand. "No, she'll be joining us later, but let me introduce you to my sister, Isolde. She's come all the way from Ireland."

Mark turned to smile at a woman of around thirty or thereabouts, who, even when tired and travel-weary, was possessed of the kind of presence that could stop people in their tracks.

"*Isolde*, is it? Well, I never! You've certainly come to the right part of the world. Welcome to the Tintagel Hotel," he said. "Can I offer you a drink? Some water, perhaps?"

She thanked him, but shook her head. "I think I'd like to have a change and then explore the place a bit, if that's all right with you?"

"Absolutely!" he boomed, and gave an imperceptible signal to one of his staff, who hurried over from where he'd been waiting in the wings. "Jake here will get you both checked in, and show you to your rooms."

He bent down and reached out a hand to ruffle Madge's head, but she gave him the cold shoulder in favour of a bowl of dog treats and water that had been laid out beside the main door for well-behaved canine guests.

"We don't usually accept dogs," he said to Isolde, with a conspiratorial air. "But, since Madge is a very special lady, we've made an exception. Luke? You'll find a dog bed and all you need laid out in your room upstairs. If there's anything else, you just let us know."

"Very kind of you, Mark."

He turned to his sister. "I have to meet with a few of our benefactors and check through some of the details ahead of tomorrow's event. Will you be all right on your own for a while?"

Isolde gave him a nudge in the ribs. "Now who's being daft? Of course, I will."

Before he could make any further comment, they were interrupted by a loud, rumbling sound overhead.

"That can't be a storm, can it?" Luke remarked. "I know the weather is looking a bit iffy over the weekend, but—"

"That'll be my nephew," Mark explained. "He's arriving by helicopter."

Rather him than me, Isolde thought, with a shudder.

"If you'll both excuse me, I'll head out to meet him," Mark said. "I hope you have a wonderful stay."

They watched him leave, then Isolde turned to her brother.

"Have you met him?" she asked.

"Who?"

"The nephew—the one who runs the hotel group."

"Oh," Luke said, and called for Madge to re-join them, which she did without complaint. "No, but I've had plenty of contact over the phone and by e-mail. He keeps a low profile, as far as I can tell, but he seems a decent bloke."

He opened his mouth to tell her something else, and then, in a flash of inspiration, snapped it shut again.

Some things were best left to be discovered.

"I'll see you in a couple of hours," he did say. "I'll be around here or in the library, if you need me."

The rumbling continued overhead, and she realised the pilot was circling the helipad.

Either that, or there was a storm coming, after all.

CHAPTER 6

Isolde couldn't say whether it was the lure of sea and sunshine, or simply relief at having left Dublin behind, but she was filled with an energy and optimism she hadn't felt in weeks. The swelling in her head had lessened considerably thanks to a short course of anti-inflammatories, and she hadn't experienced any blurred vision or cramping in her stomach since she'd arrived on Cornish soil. Buoyed by it all, and eager to shake off the cobwebs, she decided to take a walk along the headland towards the nearest beach so that she could kick off her shoes and spread her toes in the sand. She even changed into a swimsuit, which she wore beneath a pair of shorts and a loose linen shirt tied at the waist.

A quick look at the map provided by the hotel staff told her that the nearest beach was Trebarwith Strand, a couple of miles further along the headland to the west of the castle. The distance gave her a moment's pause, but she told herself that she would walk as far as possible and could always turn back if necessary. She decided to leave a message for Luke with the concierge, and then stepped out into the blazing sunshine to cross the formal gardens and pick up the coastal path that would take her where she needed to go.

The walk was idyllic, the heat of the sun tempered by a constant breeze that rolled in from the sea, and Isolde felt her spirits rise. As she passed the entrance to the castle complex, she paused to sip at a bottle of water, raising a hand to shield her eyes against the glare of the early afternoon sun. She marvelled at the splendour of jumbled ruins on the island peninsula and was tempted to abandon her beach plans and follow the pathway along with the line of tourists who made their way over the iron bridge, but she decided to save the castle for another time, perhaps early the next morning when fewer people would be around.

She continued at a steady pace along the coastal path for another mile or so, until Trebarwith Strand came into view. It was a beautiful stretch of golden sand, with aquamarine water lapping at the shoreline, where groups of swimmers and body-boarders enjoyed the ebb and flow of the tide under the watchful eye of a seasonal lifeguard. Excited to join them and feel the cool water against her skin, Isolde began to descend the long wooden staircase that hugged the cliffside and led down to the beach below.

She found a spot near the cliffs where she tucked her beach bag beneath a rock, took another long drink of water and then stripped off her outer clothing. She stood for a moment, tipped her face up to the sun, and then, with a happy laugh, jogged over the sand to join the other bathers in the water. She was a strong swimmer as a rule, so the prospect of a light swell presented no challenge to her former self.

Later, she would reflect that it was her *current* self that she should have worried about.

Standing there in the shallows, with the sun on her skin and sand tickling her toes, she felt only a deep sense of peace at the sound of the water and the laughter of families playing ball games further up the beach. She noted the flags at either end, saw that it was safe to swim within their allotted range, and took the plunge alongside many others who'd gathered there to while away a few hours during the long summer holidays.

The water was blessedly cool, and Isolde let out a long sigh of contentment as she struck out with confident strokes, smiling at those she passed by, casting an occasional glance back over her shoulder towards the beach to check that she had not veered too far away from safe waters. Happy to see that all was well, she rolled onto her back and let herself float for a while, looking up to watch the sea birds flap overhead, swooping down now and then to prey upon a fish.

Very suddenly, the skies began to change, dark clouds moving swiftly to block out the sun so that the day was no longer bright, but dull. An assessment of her own body told her that she was beginning to feel tired in any case and, knowing she needed to walk back to the hotel, she decided it was time to swim towards the beach.

When she rolled back on to her front, she was surprised to find the shoreline appeared much further away than she'd thought and that most of the crowd seemed to have vanished. Treading water, she scanned the strip of golden sand, looking for the lifeguard in his bright red and yellow uniform, but could see nothing.

The lifeguard had gone too.

Feeling unsettled, she began to swim back towards the shore in steady strokes, counting them off as she went. After a few minutes her limbs began to feel heavy, and she realised with a jolt of panic that the force of the tide was pulling her back, pushing her further and further out to sea despite all her efforts to move forwards.

She knew real fear, then, and drew upon all of her remaining resources to continue slicing through the waves, while overhead the storm that had threatened now started to gather force, washing away the blue skies of earlier. After a few minutes spent in hard exertion, she was forced to take a break, turning onto her back to rest briefly before forcing herself to begin all over again. She repeated the process several times, inching her way back towards the shore while her muscles wept, propelled forward by a sheer will to survive. As the beach drew a little nearer, she could see that that it was completely empty, and the reason was glaringly obvious.

The tide was coming in.

Something she had, clearly, been too stupid to check.

Tears mingled with the salt water as she continued to swim, pushing her body mercilessly to the brink because there was no other choice and nobody to help in the battle she waged. Another shock was in store, for she realised the riptide was not only pushing her out to sea but to the *side*, closer and closer to the rocks at the far end of the beach, well outside the area that had been designated 'safe'. Rain began to fall, lightly at first, and then in great droplets that ran down her face and splashed into her eyes.

Isolde called out then, though there was nobody to hear, and her head slid beneath the water.

She came back up, spluttering and coughing, fighting all the while against forces that felt like invisible hands dragging her down into the deep. She fought the sea, kicking out and moving her arms, but she knew that, soon, her strength would fail her.

It was only a matter of time.

Long minutes passed as she tried to keep her head above water but, when she felt those invisible hands drag her down again, she could do nothing to prevent it.

She simply had no more energy left to fight.

Seconds after her head submerged, Isolde felt a strong set of hands grasp her arms and thrust her back up to the surface. She gasped for air, coughing water from her lungs while her limbs flailed and fear of the sea, of death, and of all that had happened to her lately, overcame good sense. She began to fight the arms that held her securely, kicking out to free herself from the tide before it could drag her beneath the surface again.

Then, she heard a hard, breathless voice at her ear.

"For God's sake, *stop struggling*, and let me help you!"

The hands were real, this time, and belonged to a man whose long legs propelled them both against the tide, carving a ruthless path through the water back to shore. She heard his laboured breathing over the sound of the rain that continued to lash down, and tried to move her legs weakly to help.

"Just stay still," he puffed. "It's easier."

She did as she was told and went limp in his arms, hardly able to believe that somebody had come to help her, after all. The journey back towards land was laboured, but then, after what seemed an eternity of slow progress over the waves, his arm shifted from her shoulders to support her as they reached the shallows.

"Try to stand, if you can," he gasped, his own chest heaving in and out as he recovered from what had been an epic battle with the sea.

Isolde managed to stand on wobbly legs, shivering convulsively as she leaned against his arm and peered through the gloom. There was barely anything left of the golden beach, only a strip of sand remaining now that the tide had come in, and even that would be gone in the coming minutes. Soon, they would no longer be able to stand there, nor reach the rocks still visible at either end of the beach.

As if coming out of a trance, she turned to look at her rescuer properly, and found herself staring at a wall of muscle.

She raised her gaze a bit higher, and immediately regretted it.

His eyes might have been a deep, dark brown, but they were filled with anger.

"Thank y—" she began to say.

"Save it for later," he said. "We need to get the hell out of here, quickly, before there's no safe way out at all. Make for the rocks over there, and we can pick up the stairs to the top, if we're lucky."

He didn't wait for a response, but snatched up her cold hand and began dragging her towards the rocks nearest the cliff steps. The bottom of the staircase was no longer accessible, but, with a bit of ingenuity, they could clamber over the rocks and still reach the stairs from there, if they hurried. Already feeling like a dreadful burden, Isolde tried to keep up with his long-legged strides as they waded through the rising tide, but was almost sick with exhaustion and her legs gave way beneath her.

Without a word, he swung her up into his arms, holding her shivering body high against his chest as he carried on towards the rocks and the staircase beyond, pushing through the water which, by now, reached well above the knee. Isolde clung onto his neck, feeling humiliated by her own stupidity, as well as other emotions that had nothing whatsoever to do with almost drowning. She felt a cord of muscle in the arms that held her, heard the beat of his heart pumping at her ear, and felt a deep sense of safety in the stranger's arms that far surpassed any gratitude at having been rescued from the water.

It was like coming home.

Embarrassed by her own thoughts, she was glad when they reached the rocks and he set her down again.

"Up here," he said, pointing towards the easiest one for her to climb.

She braced her hands on the hard stone, but had no strength to lift herself up, so he gave her another helping hand—in fact, he gave her *two*—one on each cheek, as he shoved her up and out of the water.

"Wh—what do you think you're *doing*?"

She scuttled away, putting a measly distance between them while he heaved himself up onto the rock beside her.

He looked at her with open contempt. "What am *I* doing?" He laughed shortly. "I thought I was saving you from drowning or being dashed against the rocks, and then helping you find your way back to safety," he said, in a voice that dripped with sarcasm. "What were *you* doing, out there? Trying to get yourself killed? Do you have a death wish, or something?"

Her eyes narrowed into icy blue slits. "Thank you very much for helping me," she said, stiffly. "But that doesn't give you the right to help *yourself*."

He looked at her in confusion, then the penny seemed to drop. He ran a hand through his dripping hair and let it fall away again, obviously nearing the end of his patience. "That's funny," he said, in a tone that suggested it was anything but. "I don't recall you having *any* objection to having my hands on you while I was breaking my back out there, in the open water. As for 'helping myself'..."

He raked his eyes over her, unimpressed.

"Don't flatter yourself," he snapped. "I was trying to help you up onto the rocks, since you've run out of steam, that's all. Call me old-fashioned, but I prefer my women to be fully in command of themselves when I touch them, not vulnerable and shaking like a leaf. I didn't risk my own life for the promise of a cheap thrill, believe me."

The enormity of what he'd done for her hit home, and Isolde was suddenly very aware of the fact they were both dressed in scraps of material; she, in a skimpy red swimsuit cut for fashion rather than function, and he, in a pair of dark underpants that left little to the imagination, having abandoned his clothes to hurry down to the water to try and save her. He'd demonstrated extreme bravery, and she should have been thanking him.

"I'm sorry," she said.

Tears sprang to her eyes, and he swore softly.

"Forget it," he said. "Let's just get moving." He brushed past her to begin picking over the rocks, then paused to hold out a hand. "Well?" he asked. "Are you coming?"

Isolde took the hand that was offered, finding it warm despite the cold rain that continued to fall against their bare skin.

He led her over the rocks with careful steps. "What's your name, anyway?"

"Isolde," she mumbled.

He stopped dead in his tracks and turned to look at her again. "*Isolde*," he repeated, and then, to her surprise, began to laugh. "I might have known."

The action lit up his face, and she found herself smiling in return.

"I know," she said, rubbing her hands over her arms to warm them. "It's very fitting, given the old legend in these parts."

His eyes skimmed over her face. "Very fitting, indeed." Then, he tugged her hand again. "We're nearly there," he said gently. "Watch your step, though—neither of us wants to fall."

CHAPTER 7

They managed to clamber over the slippery rocks together, and Isolde was under no illusions that, without his help, it would have been an almost impossible task. He led the way, forging a path she could follow, all the while keeping a tight hold on her hand so that she wouldn't lose her footing. Eventually, they reached the edge of the beach steps where they were able to climb over the guard rail and plant their feet against something solid.

"There," he said, cheerfully. "Just a few stairs, now."

A few?

Isolde cast her eye over the staircase, which had seemed so easy on the way down, but now presented a mountain for her to climb back up again. Her muscles had been pushed to the limit, but she was mindful of the gathering wind and deepening storm clouds, not to mention the small fact that they were both frozen to the core.

"Lead on," she said decisively, and began to count each step, as she'd counted each stroke in the water.

Before her legs could give out again, they'd reached the summit.

"Made it," he declared, and looked across at the woman trailing behind him, who was paler than a ghost and looked about ready to collapse. "Where are you parked, Isolde? I could drive you home, and it might be worth getting yourself checked out, if you feel unwell—"

She swayed on the wind, teeth chattering in her mouth. "My—my bag," she managed. "It's down there, probably swept out with the tide, now. It had all of my clothes in it."

"Car keys, too?"

"No, I walked."

He raised a dark eyebrow at that. "Where from?"

"The Tintagel Hotel," she said. "It's at least two miles away from here."

"Yes, I know it," he said, and smiled. "Look, I left my clothes over there by the bench before I came down. Let's see what we can cobble together."

They hurried towards a jumble of clothing sitting crumpled and forlorn beneath one of the wooden benches overlooking the sea.

"They might not be completely dry," he said, snatching them up. "But it's better than nothing. Here, you take this."

He offered her a linen shirt, which came down to her mid-thigh, while he tugged on the chino shorts he'd discarded earlier.

"Take this, as well," he said, holding out a zip-up hoodie, which looked cosy, inviting and, most crucially, *warm*.

"Won't you be cold without anything on top?" she asked, as he continued to brave the wind rolling in from the sea with a bare chest and a stoic attitude.

"I'll manage," he said, and held out the hoodie that she could slip her arms inside.

It smelled of him, she thought. The combination of an aftershave that was pleasant without being overpowering, mingled with his own scent.

"Have my flip flops, as well," he offered, and gave her a quizzical look when she just stared at them. "What's the matter? Are you going into shock?"

"Probably," she replied, taking the sandals from him. "But, no. I just wanted to tell you again how grateful I am for everything you've done. I've never been more ashamed of myself than I am today, for the position I put us both in."

He experienced a strong, unexpected urge to hold her in his arms again, this time for the pure pleasure of it.

"Accidents happen," he said, and looked out across the sea. "I know these waters, whereas you're obviously a stranger, if your accent's anything to go by. That current can take even the strongest swimmer by surprise."

He didn't feel it necessary to mention that it had taken *him* by surprise, too, and that it had been an experience he was unlikely to forget for the rest of his life.

"Do you have a car?"

"No," he said, with regret. "I decided to come out for a walk, just like you, and didn't imagine I'd need one. I should have known the weather was liable to turn; it's mercurial."

She wondered if he was a local, and supposed he *must* be, since he'd said that he knew the waters.

Then, she wondered if there was anybody waiting for him, at home.

"The café looks closed," he was saying, and pointed to the beach café a short way off. "But I've got a phone on me, so let's hope the battery hasn't died—"

He raised it to his ear, stepped away briefly, and gave her the thumbs up while he proceeded to speak to whoever was at the other end of the line.

"Someone's coming to give us a lift," he said. "Should be less than five minutes."

She wondered how he could manage to arrange a collection so quickly, then realised he was probably friends with the local taxi driver or—

Or maybe he'd called his wife.

"—Isolde?"

"Yes?"

"I think it's best if we make our way towards the car park," he repeated. "It's easier to collect us from there."

They walked across the sodden ground together, not touching at all, and yet she'd never felt more intimate with another person than she did with the tall, enigmatic man—who, she realised with a start, was still a stranger without a name.

She turned to ask him, but was forestalled by the arrival of their transportation.

"Here we are," he said, and pointed towards one of the guest cars from the Tintagel Hotel that was pulling into the beach car park.

"That was more like three minutes," she said.

He had a quick word with the driver, then held open a door for her to step inside.

"Don't you need a lift somewhere?" she asked him.

"I have some business in Trebarwith," he said, nodding towards the little village beyond. "It's why I came out here in the first place."

She'd completely derailed his day, Isolde thought, and wished the ground would swallow her alive.

"I'm sure we'll meet again," he said. "Take care, Isolde, and try not to get into any more trouble until then."

"Wait! What's your na—"

The car door had already closed, and he was gone.

CHAPTER 8

By the time Isolde arrived back at the hotel, it was almost four o'clock. She slipped inside without attracting too much attention, although a woman dressed only in a man's shirt and a swimsuit was always going to raise a few eyebrows. She bypassed their curious stares and hurried back to her room, where she made a beeline for the bathroom and its enormous walk-in shower.

She let the hot water pummel her skin and, while it awakened her bruised muscles, it also defrosted her mind. She rested her forehead on the tiles and allowed herself to consider what might have been, before consigning it to the past. It did no good to wonder 'what if'; there was only 'what *was*'.

She recognised the danger that had been avoided, and, as luck would have it—

No, she corrected herself, with brutal honesty. It had not been 'luck' that saved her life today.

It was a man with warm brown eyes and gentle hands.

Her body tingled, a fact she put down to the hot water and residual cortisol swimming around her veins. The 'fight or flight' response could be a very powerful thing, and it was only natural that she felt as shaky as a fawn. She probably needed something to eat, that was all.

Her stomach rumbled eloquently, to reinforce the point.

Five minutes later, as she was deliberating what to wear to dinner, there came a knock at the door.

"Gabi!"

Her brother's wife was a lovely woman, with a big heart and a love of books that was second to none. Isolde had always longed for a sister, and, between Gabi and Maeve, she felt she'd been blessed with two women she considered as near as she could get to having the real thing.

"It's *so* good to see you," Gabi said, and enveloped her in a hug. "Luke told me what happened."

Isolde thought of her near drowning and realised they couldn't possibly know about that, so Gabi must be referring to the intruder incident in Dublin. In light of recent events, it had faded into insignificance.

"I've had better weeks," she said, with masterly understatement. "But, I'd rather hear all your news."

Before moving to Cornwall, Gabi had experienced her own share of traumatic events and understood all about the kind of debilitating post-traumatic stress that could take hold, if she let it. But there was a time and a place for dealing with that kind of thing and, if Isolde wasn't ready to talk about it, she would not press the issue.

"I'm here, if you need me," she said, and spied the dresses laid out on the bed. "Ooh, those are lovely, but then, you always have such nice taste. Which one are you going to wear?"

They spent some time chatting over inconsequential things while Isolde dressed and dried her hair, catching up on what had happened in their lives since they'd last seen one another, and then Gabi stood up again.

"We'd better get going," she said. "Dinner's in half an hour, but I want to introduce you to some people before then."

Isolde was an outgoing person normally, a prerequisite for a woman in her profession, but she experienced an unfamiliar frisson of nerves at the prospect of having to socialise with strangers that could only be attributed to a loss of confidence over the past few weeks.

"What happened to your arm?" Gabi asked.

Isolde looked down to find that her rescuer's grip had left a mark on her upper arms while he'd held her securely above the water.

"*Oh,*" she said. "I'll tell you all about it over dinner, but I could use a drink first."

"You're speaking my language," Gabi said, and the two women went off in search of medicinal cocktails.

A long, polished bar had been installed in one of the main reception rooms, adjacent to an enormous library stuffed with books of all descriptions. It was here that Gabi and Isolde found Luke, engaged in lively conversation with a small group of people.

"I was just about to send out a search party," he said. "Let me make some introductions."

Luke turned first to a tall man with sun-kissed brown hair and a relaxed manner, who stood with his arm around a beautiful, red-headed woman.

"Isolde, these are our friends Nick and Kate," Luke said. "They live over on the Helford with their son, Jamie, and their new addition—have you named the puppy, yet?"

"Jamie wanted to call him, 'Pokemon' but we managed to talk him out of it," Kate laughed. "We settled on 'Kurt'."

"Why Kurt?" Isolde asked.

"After the one and only Cobain," Nick replied, with a grin. "Only one of the greatest indie musicians who ever lived—"

"Don't get him started," Kate laughed, and gave him an affectionate bump with her hip. "It's a lifelong obsession."

"Of course, I remember Luke telling me you were in the music industry," Isolde said. "And Kate, I've seen some of your paintings, they're beautiful."

"Thank you," Kate said, still amazed that she was able to do the work she loved. "It's great to meet you, Isolde."

"You should see Kate's illustrations," another voice intoned, this time belonging to a man with jet black hair and—it had to be said—one of the best-looking faces she'd ever seen in real life. He stood beside an attractive woman with intelligent, watchful eyes that seemed to see through to her very soul; it was mildly disconcerting, but, when she learned that Sophie Keane was a local detective inspector in the Cornwall and Devon Police, it made sense.

"Gabriel's our local hot-shot author and newest friend in these parts," Luke provided, with a smile. "Kate's done some illustrations for his new series of children's books. This is Sophie, his fiancée, not to mention our resident murder detective, so you know who you should call if you find any dead bodies in the broom cupboard."

"I'm off duty," Sophie said, with feeling. "I've been looking forward to a weekend without any brutal murders or drunken assaults; I've left my constable to field those, while we sample the wine list."

"I'll cheers to that," Isolde said, and clinked her glass.

Talk turned to other things and, before long, she found herself laughing along with them, as if they'd known each another for years. She watched her brother's face as he regaled them with some tale or another while his wife offered some pithy one-liners in response, and found herself wondering what it would be like to have somebody special to come home to at the end of the day—somebody other than her housemate.

"So, what did you get up to this afternoon?" Luke asked.

He might have thought that she looked a bit tired, but he knew far better than to utter such blasphemy aloud.

"Well," she began, and knocked back a couple of fingers of daiquiri. "I had a bit of a…well, you could say, things got a bit *hairy* in the water down at Trebarwith Strand."

Luke had learned to read between his sister's lines long ago.

"And by 'hairy', just what are we talking about here? Shark attack? Jellyfish sting?"

Isolde decided it would be best to downplay the reality of what had happened, since he was already so worried about her wellbeing. "It was nothing, really," she lied. "I decided to go for a swim, which seemed perfectly safe since there was a lifeguard and plenty of other people out on the water. I went a bit too far out, and the swim back to shore took it out of me, that's all."

She swilled her cocktail, not meeting her brother's eye.

"Did the lifeguard help you?"

"No, they'd packed up for the day," she replied, and gestured expansively around the room. "This is a lovely place, isn't it—"

"Why did the lifeguard just leave you out there, in dangerous waters?"

Isolde realised she'd floated so far out, they might not have seen her.

"It's my own fault; I should have checked the tide times," she said. "Still, all's well that ends well."

"The current can be pretty strong around there, when the tide comes in," Nick said. "You must be a fantastic swimmer to have made it out on your own."

Isolde felt a stab of guilt. "Well, actually, a passer-by came along and helped me towards the end," she admitted, and, catching the murderous expression in her brother's eye, tried to lessen the blow. "There was no need, really. I was almost back to shore… in fact, he was a bit officious, come to think of it. I would have been absolutely *fine.* He even helped himself to a feel, while we were on the rocks—"

"He *what*?" Luke spluttered, and turned immediately to Sophie. "Maybe this bloke, whoever he is, makes it his business to roam around looking for women so he can act the hero and then cop a feel. Might be worth making a police report—"

"*No*!" Isolde burst out, realising that her attempt to downplay the incident had only thrown her from the frying pan into the fire. "Really, I'd rather just forget about it—"

She swallowed the rest of her drink, giving herself time to think.

"He was hard to describe, anyway. I can barely remember him," she rabbited on. "You know, just, pretty average…a bit forgettable—"

"Who's a bit 'forgettable'?"

The deep, male voice came from somewhere behind her right shoulder, and she recognised it instantly. With a kind of horror, Isolde turned to find her rescuer standing there wearing an amused expression, and looking extremely memorable. Rather than being bare-chested in a pair of old chino shorts, he was dressed in tailored navy trousers and a form-fitting shirt, his dark, wavy hair no longer dripping with sea water but well cut around a chiselled face. But it was his eyes that commanded her attention, for they looked at her with unconcealed mirth and she knew that he'd heard every word of the yarn she'd spun.

"I wouldn't want any of the wrong element to be harassing our lovely guests," he purred. "Especially not if they're *officious*, while they're about it."

Isolde opened her mouth to say something—anything—but no sound came out.

Gabi looked between them, sensed the tension that could be sliced with a knife, and caught her husband's eye.

Luke cleared his throat. "Isolde? Let me introduce you to the owner of the hotel," he said. "Tristan Williams. Tristan? My sister, Isolde."

"*Tristan*," she repeated, in disbelief.

"At your service," he said, and leaned forward to say in an undertone, "I told you, we'd meet again."

Before she could formulate a reply, Luke had put two and two together.

"I take it you're the ruffian who helped my sister?" he said.

"Guilty as charged," Tristan said, and gave her a look that suggested he was questioning his own judgment in having done so. "I can *assure* you, my motivations were purely honourable, and no backsides were harmed in the process."

They all laughed—even Isolde.

"I didn't want you to worry," she explained to her brother. "I was trying to downplay the incident, but...the truth is, I guess I *was* struggling a bit, and I don't know where I'd be if Mr Williams hadn't—"

"Tristan," he corrected her.

She nodded, taking in the lines of his face as the setting sun streamed through a pair of large sash windows at his back.

"I *knew* it," Luke said, interrupting the moment. "I smelled a rat when you said you'd been out swimming. You're a strong swimmer, Isolde, but you need to give yourself time to recover just now—"

He broke off, not wishing to break any confidences.

"I wish I had an older brother," Kate mused, in the brief silence that followed his outburst. "Even when they're overbearing, their hearts are in the right place."

It was enough to diffuse any remaining tension, and Luke's shoulders relaxed visibly. "Sorry," he said. "I forget, sometimes, that my little sister is a grown woman, and can look after herself."

Isolde thought that, for many years, she'd been self-sufficient and happy with the status quo. Their father and mother wouldn't know the first thing about what was happening in her life—nor Luke's, for that matter. She'd grown used to shouldering responsibility, occasionally confiding in her close friends to ease the load of day-to-day living, but there was nobody she could have turned to for help, for sanctuary, or for protection if she needed it.

Nobody other than Luke.

Even as the thought took shape in her mind, her eyes slid over to the man standing to her right.

She watched him, surreptitiously, before he turned unexpectedly and caught her eye.

It was the funniest feeling, she would later think. Hard to describe, other than a peculiar jolt of sensation, deep in her belly. To a woman of her sensibilities, it was entirely unwelcome.

Attraction, she reasoned. He probably seemed all the more desirable because he'd saved her; certainly not because of any personal attributes he might happen to possess. Added to which, she happened to have experienced a bit of a drought, lately, which could lead a person to start imagining all manner of things about perfect strangers…

"Time for dinner," he said, as though he'd read her mind.

They began to file out towards the restaurant, and Isolde took good care to leave a wide berth between herself and Tristan Williams. In the end, she needn't have worried, because he was waylaid by one of the young waitresses behind the bar who asked to speak to him. The girl in question was very pretty, somewhere in her early twenties with large blue eyes—she couldn't say why it irritated her so much, especially since she was blonde and blue-eyed herself—and, in any case, what did it matter what one of his employees looked like? Thoroughly annoyed with herself, she turned away, but not before she watched Tristan approach the bar and lean forward so that he could speak to the woman, their heads close together in hushed conversation.

She wondered if their discussion was entirely to do with business.

Which, of course, was none of hers.

CHAPTER 9

Tristan joined them in the hotel restaurant a few minutes later and, as he approached their table, she realised that the only unoccupied seat was opposite hers. His face gave away no indication that he'd noticed, nor that he cared; in fact, if she wasn't mistaken, he bore a troubled expression that hadn't been there earlier in the evening nor even when they'd dragged themselves out of the sea.

"Thank you again, Tristan, for opening your doors for the auction," Luke said affably.

The other man waved it away. "No trouble," he said, though it must have been.

"People have been so generous," Gabi remarked. "We've got everything from paintings to boats, to writing classes with a bestselling author and sessions with a world-famous record producer—"

She smiled at Nick and Gabriel, who were seated further along the table.

"I thought about offering a 'Get out of Jail Free' card, but unfortunately that's frowned upon by my superiors," Sophie said.

"There would probably have been a stampede," Isolde laughed.

"And what are you planning to offer for the auction?" Tristan said softly, catching her off-guard.

"Ah—well, I don't know. I'm not sure what I *could* offer."

"I know," Kate said. "What about a masterclass in journalism and public relations? Loads of people attending tomorrow are heads of local businesses, but they're not all adept at speaking on camera or handling interviews. You could offer a few sessions, or something of that kind?"

There was a general murmur of agreement.

"What do you say?" Luke asked. "You shouldn't feel any pressure though; we have more than enough to auction off."

But Isolde shook her head. “I’m happy to,” she decided. “Especially as it’s for such a good cause.”

“I didn’t know journalism was your line,” Tristan said. “Do you work for a newspaper?”

“No, I work for a broadcaster.”

“Isolde is being modest,” Gabi told him. “She’s the main news anchor for the whole of Ireland.”

Surprise flickered briefly in his eyes, before the teasing look returned. “Very impressive,” he said. “Do you enjoy it?”

The question was harmless enough, and he wasn’t to know that she’d been forced to take some time off work, nor any of the reasons why. However, he must have noticed the sadness pass over her face, for he changed the subject immediately.

“How about some water?”

“Thank you,” she said. “Why don’t you tell me about the hotel business?”

He leaned forward, and, for a moment, she might have believed they were the only two people at the table.

“It was my father’s business, really,” he began. “When he died, he left it to my mother and me, and we ran it together for a while. When she’d had enough, she asked if I'd take the helm, which I was happy to do."

"Do you enjoy it?" she asked, echoing his own question.

"Nobody has ever really asked me that before," he replied, and gave the question serious thought. "I suppose it's all I've known, but, yes, I do enjoy it. The work is varied and there's a lot of travel, although I'm mostly based out of New York."

Her stomach fell, and, mistaking the feeling for hunger, she grabbed a bread roll. "It's a great city," she said.

"It's true what they say about it never sleeping," he replied. "When I was younger, I used to love that aspect. Lately, I've started to question whether it would be nice to put down more permanent roots, somewhere with a slightly less frenetic pace of life."

She looked up to find him watching her.

"I grew up here," he continued. "My mother and father were busy, but this was always our home. I'd like to create something similar for my family, one day."

"Are you married?" The question fell out of her mouth before she could prevent it, and a blush crept over her skin.

His eyes crinkled at the corners. "No," he said simply. "But I'm always hopeful. Are you?"

She was flustered, though she was the one who'd started that line of questioning.

"*No*, and I don't have any plans to be. I don't need to be shackled to someone for the rest of my life, just to please society."

Tristan took a thoughtful sip of his wine, then set it down again.

"I never deal in absolutes," he said. "Perhaps you shouldn't, either. Not everybody sees marriage as a way of shackling another person; for some people, it's an expression of their love and commitment."

Before she could think of a reply to that, he checked his watch, muttered an expletive, and rose suddenly to his feet.

"I'm sorry, I lost track of the time—there's somewhere I need to be."

They bade him farewell, and he left with a promise not to miss the auction the following day. The conversation continued, and good food was served, but whenever Isolde looked across at the empty chair, she felt bereft. She was also curious about where he'd been in such a tearing rush to get to, although she'd sooner have carved out her own tongue than admit as much.

Projection, she thought. *That's what was happening to her.*

She'd heard about people forming silly romantic crushes on the person who'd rescued them; in fact, she'd once interviewed a woman who was convinced she'd fallen in love with the fireman who'd rescued her from a house fire, even though he hadn't reciprocated the feeling and was, in fact, happily married with four children at home.

Besides, Tristan Williams was hardly her type.

And who would be your type, Isolde? A good-looking, successful, intelligent, kind and brave sort of man who spoke easily of marriage and family?

There was no answer to that, so she reached for another bread roll.

Danielle Teague didn't intend to be a waitress all her life.

Hospitality was one of the main sources of employment for young people in Cornwall, with the many bars, hotels and restaurants hiring seasonal staff to turn down beds and make sure the up-country visitors were taken care of sufficiently that they would return the following year. At twenty-four, she felt she'd already outstayed her welcome in that industry, and her dreams of travelling the world were slipping further out of reach with every passing summer. The Tintagel Hotel was certainly the best employer she'd ever had, but it was small consolation to a girl who wanted bigger and better things.

Fate had other plans.

Thoughts of travel and dreams of success were far from Danielle's mind as she awakened in the pitch darkness, her body cold and crumpled on a hard floor. As she came around, head aching and stomach churning, she spread her hands and realised she was lying on wet, compacted sand. She tried to stand, clutching a hand to her head, which was aching and sore. Feeling her way through the darkness, she almost walked straight into a rocky wall to her left, so she turned in the other direction and did the same thing again, this time cracking her forehead against the rough edge of a rocky wall to her right.

A tunnel?

Crying out in pain, she crouched back down onto all fours and began to crawl towards the sound of the waves, hoping it would take her out onto the beach so that she could make her way back to the hotel and find help. The ground angled downhill and she moved slowly, sharp little rocks puncturing her skin from time to time and then—

She tumbled forward, falling down into the darkness with a shriek that was swallowed by a mouthful of seawater. The shock of cold water took her breath away, but it was nothing to the waves that sloshed around the cave, tossing her back and forth, threatening to take her down.

Suddenly, she knew where she was.

Williams Cave.

It passed directly beneath the hotel, and was accessible from Haven Beach at low tide, when there was only a sandy floor, but when the tide came in it filled with water and was completely impassable. By her reckoning, she was already inside, and the tide was coming in fast, crashing against the cave walls.

Through the generations, tunnels had been built for smugglers to use when bringing in their contraband, including one which ran from Williams Cave up into the Tintagel Hotel, which must have been the rocky corridor where she'd awakened.

Terrified by the force of the sea, and the all-consuming darkness, Danielle hurried to retrace her steps, dragging herself out of the freezing water so that she could scramble back up the rocky incline towards the tunnel's entrance. It was an effort, but she made it, and now that her eyes had adjusted to the meagre light, she could see the entrance. She hurried, feet skidding over the rocks, arms held wide for balance.

She walked carefully back across the hard sand, through the blackened entrance to the tunnel, past the point where she had lain.

And then, stopped abruptly.

An old iron gate stood in her way.

She grasped the metal bars and rattled them, tugging the gate with all her might, but it wouldn't budge. Her fingers felt their way, looking for the lock so that she could check for a key, but there was only a single padlock and no key left inside.

Just then, the first splash of seawater reached her ankles, the tide having risen high enough to enter the tunnel. Danielle cried out, shouting for help until her voice was raw, but the sound was lost on the wind.

She had two choices: to stay where she was, and wait for the sea to reach her there in the narrow tunnel, where she would surely drown; or, to try swimming again, but the sea level was already dangerously high and its current deadly, and she would also surely drown or be smashed against the cave walls. Either way, she faced death, and the knowledge of it was enough to loosen her bowels.

There would be no travelling the world for Danielle Teague.

CHAPTER 10

Saturday morning

The day dawned brightly for the residents of the Tintagel Hotel, the sun spreading wide arcs of hazy light over the cliffs and touching the old stone walls with its gentle rays. Isolde had found it difficult to settle in her bed during the long hours of the night, while snatched memories of being underwater mingled with the face of a dark intruder, chasing away any promise of sleep. When the morning sunshine shone through her window, it helped to wash away the nightmares, offering hope for a new day which she grasped with both hands.

After a quick shower, she met Luke, Gabi and Madge out on the terrace for breakfast, where she ordered a 'Full Cornish' and a pot of hot water.

"Just hot water?" her brother enquired. "Don't tell me you're on one of these weird diets."

"Hardly, since I just ordered a full breakfast with all the works," Isolde laughed. "The water is for my tea. I brought my own blend," she explained. "There's a Chinese herbalist near where we live, and Maeve brought back a calming blend for me—I think it has camomile, ginseng and a few other things that are good for the nervous system."

"Oh, how kind of her," Gabi said. "Can I try some?"

"I'll stick to coffee, thanks," Luke said, and both women had to laugh at his look of distaste. "Never could stand herbal tea."

"How is Maeve?" Gabi asked.

"She's well, as far as I know," Isolde replied, although it occurred to her that she hadn't heard from her friend since she'd left Dublin, which was unusual. "After the incident at the house, she's been staying with her parents for a couple of days, but I know she was planning to move back in today, so I'll try giving her a call later."

"She's been a good friend to you," Luke said.

"Yes, she has. It can be difficult to find friends in the same industry, with so much competition and back-stabbing around, but we've never suffered from any of that. I'm lucky to have found her."

"When you find a good friend, hold onto them." Gabi smiled, and reached a hand down to ruffle Madge's head, the dog having heard the words 'Full Cornish' and come to investigate.

"It's hard to believe there was a storm yesterday," Isolde remarked. "The sky is the most beautiful shade of blue."

"That's how it begins," Gabi said. "Unfortunately, there's an amber weather warning for this evening. We were just discussing whether we should postpone the auction."

"I don't think we need to cancel the whole event," Luke said, having polished off his bacon sandwich. "Half the time, these reports are exaggerated."

"Most of the people will be arriving today," Gabi explained, for Isolde's benefit. "Even if the weather takes a turn for the worse, I can't imagine it would be bad enough to stop people from travelling home early, if they need to."

"I could have a bus driver on standby, as a precaution," Luke decided. "It was rattling the walls so much, last night, it sounded like somebody was screaming in torment."

"I thought I'd dreamed that," Isolde said, and offered Gabi a cup of tea. "You're right, it must have been the wind. It was really howling."

"It all adds to the *atmosphere* of the place," Gabi said, in a dramatic voice.

"You can tell which one of us likes reading murder mysteries," Luke said, with an affectionate smile for his wife.

"I keep saying we should put on a murder mystery weekend," she replied. "You know, get a few actors in, have everybody dress up and play a part while they try to figure out who the killer is? It would be a real hoot."

"So long as it's not the real thing, that's fine with me," Luke said, and polished off his coffee. "I've got to supervise the hanging of some paintings this morning. Are you going to do something nice—which doesn't involve swimming in a tidal bay?"

Isolde rolled her eyes. "You're never going to let me forget that, are you?"

"Nope," he said, succinctly. "At least, not for the next forty years. After that, my memory might fail me."

"Well, that's something to look forward to," Isolde chuckled, and then turned to her sister-in-law. "Do you fancy wandering down to the castle? I haven't seen it properly, yet."

"Love to," Gabi said. "It's a nice walk, if you don't mind heights? We can bring Madge."

Isolde had never experienced any particular fear of heights before, so she shook her head. "It's a plan."

The walk to Tintagel Castle took no time at all, and the two women strolled in companionable silence for a while, the dog trotting happily ahead of them, until Gabi asked the question that was uppermost in her mind.

"How are you feeling?"

Isolde pushed her sunglasses up onto her nose, and answered as honestly as she could.

"Physically, I feel better than I have in weeks," she replied. "I'd been having problems with my vision, migraines, and stomach cramps, none of which I've had since being over here. I don't know how to explain it, except, maybe the doctor was right. Perhaps I was more stressed than I knew."

Gabi nodded. "It's great to hear that you're doing better on that score," she said. "But what about the break-in? Have you heard anything further from the police?"

"Not a peep," Isolde said. "I don't expect to, either. The person wore gloves, their entire body and face was covered, and there were no other witnesses besides me. Tracking them down will be like trying to find a needle in a haystack."

"I still can't understand why they would break in and not take anything," Gabi muttered. "It's like they were trying to scare you."

"That's what Maeve said, too. I do get a bit of hate mail, sometimes," Isolde confessed. "Mostly, the fan mail is very good, but occasionally it can be bad, especially if I'm reporting on politics or foreign policy. People can have very extreme, dogmatic views on things, and they see me as a mouthpiece for information they don't like hearing."

"I never considered that you'd be dealing with hate mail," Gabi said. "Do you think the intruder was one of those people?"

"I've considered it. The intruder just didn't seem like the average thief on the make. It felt far more personal than that. They wanted to intimidate me and, unfortunately, they succeeded."

"That depends on your point of view," Gabi said, and linked her arm through Isolde's. "A lot of people wouldn't have been able to get on a plane and come over here, let alone be able to converse easily with a group of strangers so soon after suffering all that. You're a strong person, Isolde, never forget it."

They walked a little further, until they came to one of the viewing benches, where they paused to sit and look out across the castle and the sea beyond.

"I frightened myself, yesterday," Isolde said. "I was excited to have a burst of energy. I saw everybody else swimming in the sea, and I wanted to be part of it…to feel *alive* again. I never imagined it would backfire so badly."

"I always find it best not to dwell on the past," Gabi said, and reached for a packet of paracetamol tablets she'd squirreled away in her bag. "A bit of a headache, this morning," she explained. "Must be the cocktails, from last night."

Isolde nodded. "I have a slight headache, myself."

"Anyway," Gabi continued, after offering Isolde some pain relief. "There's nothing wrong with wanting to be back to your old self, and you weren't to know about that tidal beach. You need to stop beating yourself up, so much—take it from one who knows."

Isolde knew the story of what had happened to Gabi while she'd been living in London. A former commissioning editor for a large publishing house, she'd been pushed onto the tracks of the Underground one night on her way home from an industry party and, against all the odds, had managed to survive. Her life in London had been tainted irrevocably, and she'd taken the job as manager of the little bookshop in Carnance to get away from it all, which is where she'd met Luke.

"Take all the time you need," Gabi advised. "Let your heart and mind heal at their own pace."

"I don't know how," Isolde said. "I keep having these nightmares, and, sometimes, this feeling of panic comes over me—" She trailed off.

"Well, it's an alternative therapy," Gabi mused, "but I hear that the opposite sex can be a wonderful distraction."

Isolde glanced at her, then away again. "I don't have time for men in my life," she said. "And, in any case, who would I find out here?"

Gabi gave her a long look. "I think you and I both know you've already found someone who piques your interest," she said, wickedly. "If you ask me, he'd be the *ideal* distraction."

As if she'd conjured him from the skies above, Tristan appeared on the pathway, dressed simply in faded jeans and a white t-shirt that made Isolde think unaccountably of Diet Coke.

"Did you tell him we'd be here?" she hissed.

"Certainly not," Gabi said, but made a note to thank her husband for doing her bidding. "Morning, Tristan!"

He crossed the grass to join them, and crouched down to give Madge a scratch between the ears.

"Good morning," he said. "Beautiful day, isn't it? Makes you want to reach out and grab it."

"We were just saying the same thing," Gabi replied, sweetly. "In fact, we were going to head down to the castle for a look around, if you'd like to join us?"

"Why not?"

The three of them walked the remaining distance to the entrance of the castle complex before Gabi dealt her final card without a scrap of sisterly remorse.

"Oh, *darn*," she said, and snapped her fingers. "I forgot; I need to get back to help Luke with something. You two enjoy yourselves, and I'll see you later. C'mon Madge!"

She gave neither of them a chance to protest, and they watched her retreating back with twin expressions of amusement.

"Well," he said, and cleared his throat.

"Well," she agreed.

"Shall we see this castle?" he offered.

"You don't have to come," Isolde said quickly. "You must have plenty of other things to do."

"Yes, but there's nothing I'd rather do."

She smiled. "So long as I'm not keeping you from anything important?"

"The bridge is this way," he said, and steered her along a pathway which took them past a large bronze sculpture depicting a male figure wearing a crown and carrying a sword.

"Is that King Arthur?" she asked. "It's beautiful."

"Many people think it's Arthur, but actually it's called 'Gallos'. It was supposed to represent the general history of the site, because, in reality, Tintagel was probably a summer residence for the old kings of Cornwall, rather than the Knights of the Round Table."

"You should work for the Tourist Board," she said, with a smile. "Have you always been a fan of local history?"

"All kinds of history," he said. "If I hadn't become a hotelier, I'd have been a teacher."

She could hardly imagine it. "There's still time, yet," she said. "I'm a willing student, so, tell me, was there always a bridge spanning the peninsula here, or has the rock eroded away?"

"Do you really want to know?"

"I really want to know."

"All right, then," he said, and pretended to roll up his sleeves. "In the Middle Ages, there was always a bridge crossing here. It disappeared sometime during the fourteenth and seventeenth centuries, I think. The castle is cared for by English Heritage, and they built this bridge in iron and slate back in 2019 to make it easier for people to get across."

"How would they cross the peninsula otherwise?" she asked.

"There's another route, lower down the cliffs, but it's a network of narrow pathways with over a hundred steps," he said. "It was difficult for some people to traverse, so they reinstated the original route."

Soon, they came to the footbridge, which was situated at the highest point of the cliffs. It spanned a distance of one hundred and ninety feet across the gorge and a similar height above sea level, so Tristan told her, and the effect was that it seemed to hang in mid-air.

"Do you want to go across first, or would you rather I did?" he asked.

"I'll go," she said, with more enthusiasm than she felt.

Isolde gripped the edge of the handrail and took the first couple of steps before she was forced to stop, feeling her head spin and her heart quicken. The wind rushed against her face and through the balustrades, buffeting the steelwork, and although she knew it had been built soundly and was perfectly safe, her feet refused to move any further forward.

"I'm sorry, Tristan, but I don't think I can cross the bridge today," she said. "I don't know what's the matter with me—"

"There's no need to explain," he said, and held out his hand to help her step off. "This bridge isn't for everyone, especially when it's a bit windy. We can easily take the steps down to The Haven and come up on the other side."

She took his hand, and they began to make their way down the path. "What's The Haven?"

"Some people call it Castle Cove," he said. "It's the name of the beach down there, on the north side of the peninsula. For years, slate from the quarries around Tintagel was transported to the cliffs above it, where it was transferred onto derricks and let down to beach level, where it was then loaded onto beached ships that had been towed in from the open water. You can still see one of the old derricks, now."

"Sounds like a lot of work," she said, as the beach itself came into view. It was a secretive spot, she thought, where smugglers could roam without being seen from above. "How did they tow the ships in?"

"With difficulty, I should imagine," he said. "There's a cave down there, known as Merlin's Cave, which spans the whole width of the peninsula. There's also a secret passage down there on the cliffs. It leads up to the hotel."

Isolde was intrigued. "Have you ever been inside?"

"Not lately," he replied, keeping his eyes on the pathway ahead. "I remember exploring it when I was a boy, but that's such a long time ago now I've forgotten it completely. The tunnel was used for smuggling, so I'm told. The Williams family haven't always been so law-abiding."

She laughed, and looked back over her shoulder towards the hotel. "Is the passageway still open?"

"Probably," he replied. "It's accessed from behind a hidden panel in one of the cupboards beneath the stairs in the hotel, so it's highly unlikely anyone except family would know where to find it. But I mean to go down one day and check that the iron gate is locked from the inside—we couldn't risk having any curious guests getting lost down there, especially as the cave is a tidal one. If anyone was to become trapped for any reason, they'd struggle to get out again. But the tide's out now, so it's perfectly safe to have a look around after we've been to the castle, if you like."

They followed the network of steps leading down to the bottom of the gorge crossing, before they rose up again on the other side of the causeway, towards the castle. They passed through the ruins, marvelling at the scenery all around the peninsula, until Tristan wandered off a short way to inspect an engraved stone that was sunk into the grass. Isolde joined him, and crouched down to read the inscription:

Once at Tintagel
King Mark and Iseult are married,
but she often meets Tristan in the castle garden
when everyone else is asleep.

"This area was the castle garden," he said, coming to stand beside her. "Where Tristan would meet Iseult."

She stood up again and turned to face him, summoning the courage to say what she needed to say. "I want to thank you again," she said, seriously. "I behaved badly, yesterday, in more ways than one, which is out of character for me. I wanted to explain why."

He waited for her to continue.

"When you joined us in the bar, you must have caught the end of my story," she said. "I was trying to spin a tale that was less worrying, for my brother's sake, because he's already quite concerned about me—"

"Why?" he interjected.

"It's not important—"

"It's important to me."

She looked up, and found his eyes warm and understanding. "There was a break-in, at my house in Dublin," she said, and went on to tell him far more than she'd intended. "I'd already been signed off work that day, so it came as a double blow."

He listened, not moving nor speaking, but giving her his full attention.

"Luke feels responsible—I know he does, even though I'm a grown woman and we lead separate lives," she said. "I didn't want to add to his burden by telling the full truth about what happened at Trebarwith Strand yesterday, and I know that was dishonest of me, so I'm sorry for that. In my defence, I thought I'd never see you again, and that you'd never know the difference."

He grinned. "Your face was a picture in the bar yesterday," he admitted. "Even more so than now, with the light dancing in your eyes."

The atmosphere between them shifted as he took a step forward—not to crowd her, but to make his intention known.

"Thank you for explaining your motivations, Isolde," he said quietly. "As far as I'm concerned, it's behind us. I have a tough skin, in any case."

Her eyes moved to the skin on his arms and hands, and her body remembered how they'd felt as he held her, prompting her mind to wonder what they'd feel like now they were safely on dry land.

"As for what's happened to you, lately, I'm sorry to hear it," he continued, speaking softly, weaving a spell around her with his voice. "I'd ask whether the police have it in hand, but I suppose your brother has already quizzed you thoroughly about all that?"

She laughed. “Yes, I don’t need another brother—”

“The last thing I want to be is your brother.”

The tension grew heavy, as they stood there amongst the ruins of a mediaeval garden built for their namesakes.

“What would you want to be?” she whispered.

“Why don’t I show you?” Very gently, he raised his hands to cup her face, and then lowered his own until their lips were almost touching. “Am I giving you a clue?” he said.

She closed the gap between them, brushing her lips against his while her arms wrapped around his neck. He caught her up against him and they remained there for long minutes, entirely in their own world.

“You’re right,” she said, once they drew apart. “That wasn’t very brotherly.”

“Good,” he muttered, and tugged her against him again.

CHAPTER 11

Tristan and Isolde spent another hour exploring the landscape, their hands entwined as they wandered along The Haven and through the long, eerie cave made famous by Tennyson, who'd written of Merlin saving a baby Arthur from the waves and bringing him to safety inside the bowels of the rock. As they moved through the cavernous space, the sand beneath their toes was still wet from the tide that had gone out sometime during the night, and Isolde shivered.

"It's silly," she whispered. "But, I swear, this place feels haunted."

"Why are you whispering?" he whispered back.

"I don't know," she said, and laughed at herself. "It felt appropriate."

"I wouldn't have pegged you as a believer in ghosts and ghouls," he said, but was happy for an excuse to wrap his arm around her. "It's such an ancient part of the world, I suppose it's impossible not to think of all the footsteps that have gone before ours, all the men and women who might have hidden in here—"

"Or died in here," she whispered again. "You said yourself, the tide can be a killer."

By then, they'd reached the other side of the cave and emerged back out into the sunshine, which was beginning to disappear behind a thick layer of clouds, just as Luke and Gabi had feared. They walked a little further along The Haven, staying close to the cliffs, and then dipped inside another cave that was far smaller than Merlin's, and closer to the waterline.

"The tunnel leading to the hotel is in here," he said, keeping her close as their eyes adjusted once more to the darkness, and then he pointed towards a spot higher up the cave's wall. "There—that's the entrance."

Isolde peered through the shadows and could see what appeared to be a black hole, made inaccessible by an old iron gate blocking the entrance.

"Not easy to get to," she said, looking at the slippery incline of worn rock leading up to it.

"Now you can see why it's a good idea to keep the gate locked," he said. "When the water washes through here, it fills the cave completely, so it's just as dangerous as Merlin's Cave."

"Has anyone ever been trapped in here?"

"It wouldn't surprise me," he said. "Come on, let's get back to the hotel before your brother misses you, and puts me back on the watch list."

They headed back out into the daylight and began walking towards the stairs that would take them back up to the hotel.

"How are you feeling, after yesterday?" he asked.

Isolde had never felt better—aside from the slight hangover that rattled around her skull. "Aside from a couple of nightmares, I'm feeling pretty good," she said. "I was convinced I heard screaming during the night, but it was just my imagination."

"It'll pass," he said, and reached for her hand in silent support. "It was a good idea to come for a walk on the beach today, to wash away yesterday's memory with a better one."

"Yesterday wasn't all bad," she said.

"Oh?"

"My dreams weren't all bad, either," she found the courage to say.

Tristan smiled. "I had a restless night, too," he said softly. "My dreams had nothing to do with the sea and everything to do with the nymph I dragged out of it."

Isolde stopped walking and turned to look at him, studying the angles and shadows of his face that were new to her, and yet so familiar. She decided it was time for a sanity check.

"Tristan?"

"Mm?"

"You know that whatever is happening between us is impossible, don't you?"

"Nothing is impossible."

"We've known each other less than twenty-four hours," she argued. "I live in Dublin, and you live in New York. What are you *hoping* for?"

He turned and held her loosely in his arms.

"If you'd asked me that question two days ago, I'd have said I have everything I need in life," he said quietly. "Now, I realise a crucial part of it may be missing, and I suspect that part might be you."

"You can't talk like that," she said, pushing away from him. "You hardly *know* me, and I can tell you right now, I'm not some kind of romantic idiot—"

A vision of herself watching *Pride and Prejudice* for the umpteenth time popped into her head, making a mockery of her own statement.

She thrust it away and ploughed on.

"Let's be sensible," she began again, as he continued to stand there listening attentively to her tirade. "The most we can hope for is a fun weekend together. Then, at the end of it, you'll go your way and I'll go mine, and we'll have some great memories."

"Let's see how it goes," he said, with infuriating calm. "You'd be amazed what can be accomplished in the space of a weekend."

"Tristan—"

"Isolde?"

"Has anybody ever told you, you're infuriating?"

"Frequently," he replied, good-naturedly. "You'll get used to it."

"You're very sure of yourself, aren't you?"

He looked across at her, then back along the beach. "Actually, I've never felt less sure of myself than I do now," he replied. "I feel like I've fallen into deep water without even realising it, and I'm out of my depth." He gave her a rueful smile, and started walking again. "Do you have this effect on people often?"

She swallowed. "It's just projection," she said, in her best newsreader's voice. "You must have heard of it."

"Sure, I have," he said, as they continued along the beach. "It's the idea that someone would develop feelings for a person who's helped them or rescued them in some way, isn't it?"

"Yes, but it could work in the reverse, as well," she said. "I don't know...a bit like Florence Nightingale falling for one of her patients during the Boer War, or maybe it's the other way around. Anyway, that's probably what you're feeling for me."

"You've given this some thought," he remarked. "Is that because you've been suffering the same ailment?"

"I—that's not the point!"

He laughed, and grabbed her hand to swing her in a wide arc back into his arms. "Did anybody ever tell you, you think too much? Why not see where life takes you?"

Thoughts of her parents swam into her mind's eye, of them laughing and dancing together during the good times, before things changed. She'd spent her adult life avoiding anyone that could cause heartbreak, but, as she stood there on the beach with a man who seemed to understand her more than any other she'd ever met, Isolde asked herself whether she'd been a coward all those years. Never trusting anyone, fully; never allowing a relationship to progress, for fear she would be hurt; and, never, ever allowing herself to fall in love.

"I'm frightened," she admitted.

"Me too," he surprised her by saying. "What should we do about it?"

Isolde looked back up towards the hotel. "We've got some time before the auction begins," she said.

His eyes gleamed. "Race you to the top," he said, and set off towards the beach steps at a run.

After a second's pause, she picked up her heels and ran across the sand after him, laughter bubbling in her throat as she let memories of the past float away with the tide.

CHAPTER 12

Whatever plans they'd had for the afternoon were interrupted by Tristan's uncle, who pulled him aside as soon as they stepped into the lobby area.

"Tristan? Do you have a moment?"

He expelled a heavy sigh, and turned to Isolde.

"I'm sorry about this, but I do need to speak to him about a few things," he said. "Will you hold the thought for later?"

"I'm here all weekend," she quipped.

"I won't be long," he promised her. "I just have a couple of things to take care of."

"Take your time," she said.

Tristan watched her leave, then dragged himself back to business, following his uncle through a side door into the manager's office.

"What's up?"

"I wondered if you'd had a chance to sign off those papers we were talking about?"

Tristan shook his head. "Not yet. I need some time to go through them and look at the accounts, while I'm at it."

"I'll have them ready for you," Mark said.

"Incidentally, have you seen Danielle?"

"Danielle?"

"Danielle Teague, the waitress," Tristan prompted.

"*Oh*, Danielle, of course. No, I can't say I have. Why do you ask?"

"She was supposed to be working the morning shift, but never turned up."

"Well, the summer staff can be a bit unreliable," Mark said, and twiddled a biro between his fingers. "It's been that way for the past few years, and it doesn't help that there aren't as many young people coming over from the EU now."

Tristan knew all about it, but deferred to his uncle as a matter of politeness.

"I'm sure she'll turn up again," Mark continued. "In the meantime, we have enough staff to cover the shortfall.

Tristan stuck his hands in his pockets. "Some of the staff live on site, in the staff quarters, don't they? Is Danielle one of them?"

"I think so, but I can check..." Mark pulled up a document on his computer, then nodded. "Yes, she is."

Tristan knew that the staff who were employed with living quarters earned the best deal, often being paid over the market rate without having to pay out any living expenses of their own. It was a rare offer in Cornwall, and he would be surprised if Danielle had found a better situation elsewhere.

"Never mind," he said. "It's probably nothing."

Mark nodded, and spread his hands. "Well? You never told me what you think of the old place?"

"It's looking great," Tristan said, and didn't bother to mention the various snags he'd noted in some of the bathrooms, for it could wait until another day.

"Your mother is here," Mark said. "She asked me to tell you she'll be in the library."

"That was always Dad's favourite room," Tristan said, with a smile that was tinged with sadness. "She feels close to him there."

"We all do," Mark said, thinking of his older brother who'd passed away a couple of years before. "It's been hard not having Harry here with us."

For Tristan, the pain of his father's loss was still too raw to talk about. "I'll take a look at that paperwork shortly," he said. "See you at the auction, later."

He turned to leave, but his uncle's voice halted him. "Tristan? I know it's been some years since we spent any real, quality time together," Mark said. "But, I want you to know, I'm here if you ever need me. Your father was my greatest friend, and I hope to be yours, one day."

Tristan gave him a lopsided smile, and tried to find the similarities between Harry Williams and his younger brother. Thc two men had been born a decade apart, Harry to his grandfather's first wife and, following her untimely death, Mark to his grandfather's second wife. Though the brothers were only 'half' blood relations, they'd never made any distinction, and had remained close until

Harry's death. That being said, they were different in both looks and temperament, his father having always been a quiet, thoughtful man, whilst Mark tended to be more extrovert, which made him an ideal person to manage staff and deal with residents.

"Thanks," he said. "I might just take you up on that."

Tristan turned to leave, then paused with his hand on the door.

"You don't happen to be any good at reading women's minds, do you?"

Mark's eyebrows flew into his receding hairline.

"Well," he said, puffing his cheeks out. "I suppose I wasn't half bad, in my day, but I'd have to say the fairer sex has always remained a mystery to me."

"That's what I thought," Tristan said. "Not to worry—I'll muddle through this particular mystery on my own."

Isolde ordered an iced coffee for herself in the library bar, and settled down in a leather wingback chair positioned beside one of the windows. She was considering whether to select one of the books from the surrounding shelves, when she was interrupted by the arrival of a woman she'd never met before.

"Hello," she said, in friendly tones. "Do you mind if I park myself beside you here? All of the best spots are taken."

"Of course," Isolde said, and shifted so that the newcomer could manoeuvre her wheelchair more easily into the vacant space.

The lady, who was a youthful seventy or thereabouts, settled herself and then ordered a glass of white wine from the waiter, who came to take her order immediately. Once that was done, she looked across at the younger woman and smiled.

"Don't let me interrupt you," she said. "I'm just waiting for my son to arrive."

Isolde smiled in return. "It's no interruption," she said. "Have you just arrived?"

"Oh, yes, I'm here for the charity auction this evening. Are you here for the same event?"

"Yes, my brother arranged it."

"*Ah*," the other woman said, and realised she must be Luke Malone's sister. "I should introduce myself—I'm Meghan, but most people call me Meg."

"Isolde."

"What a beautiful name. The old legend was always one of my favourites, even if it doesn't have the happiest of endings." She took a sip, studying Isolde with a pair of deep, dark brown eyes that missed very little. "Are you enjoying your stay?"

"Very much," Isolde replied. "In fact, the owner of the hotel just gave me a guided tour of the castle and The Haven, along with Merlin's Cave and Williams Cave."

"That sounds lovely," Meg said, with a twinkle in her eye. "What do you make of him?"

"He's..." Isolde thought of Tristan, and hardly knew where to begin. "He saved my life, yesterday."

It was the first Meg had heard of it, but then, her son wasn't the kind of man to brag about his endeavours.

"That was brave," she said, and Isolde nodded.

"He's also attractive, intelligent, and he makes me smile. Frankly, I don't know what to do about it, because we live thousands of miles apart. It can't go anywhere beyond this weekend." Isolde stopped, and laughed self-consciously. "On the other hand, he makes me feel *alive*, more than anyone else I've ever known. Does that make sense?"

Meg smiled, and decided it was time to come clean. "I know exactly what you mean," she said, softly. "I felt very much the same, when I met Tristan's father, Harry."

Isolde's eyes widened.

Meg and Harry, she remembered now.

"Oh, my goodness—you're not his mother?"

"For my sins," Meg chuckled.

"I hope I haven't given any offence?"

"By telling me that you find my son attractive and intelligent? Certainly not—in fact, it's music to an old woman's ears, and gives me hope that his father and I taught him well."

Isolde could see the resemblance, now. Tristan and his mother shared the same high cheekbones, the same dark eyes and line of nose, as well as an apparent knack for catching her off guard.

"When did you two meet?"

"I've only known him a day," Isolde said. "Less than that, really."

Meg reached across the table to squeeze her hand. "Sometimes, a day is all it takes. Just think of these books," she said, gesturing around the shelves. "If you're anything like me, you'll know by the end of the first page whether you want to carry on reading. It's the same with people, I've always found. First impressions count for a lot, although society tells us we shouldn't trust them."

"I wasn't expecting to meet anyone," Isolde said, hardly understanding why she was confiding her thoughts to his mother, of all people, except that she was far too easy to talk to.

"Whoever does?" Meg asked. "Let me give you some free advice, if I may. *Nobody* is ever prepared when they meet somebody special. In fact, some people don't even realise when they do, and later live to regret it. My advice is not to be one of those people, walking blindly through life, unable to see past the things that have hurt them before. If the two of you have forged a connection, however quickly, then give it the chance it deserves, or you may live to regret it."

"And if it doesn't work out?" Isolde whispered.

"That's life," Meg replied. "We recover and move on, but without the regret of never having tried."

Words to live by, Isolde thought.

If only she had the courage.

"There he is now," Meg said, pointing out of the window. "He's out on the terrace. Would you mind being a dear, and fetching him for me?"

Isolde glanced outside and, sure enough, there was Tristan making his way back from the direction of the staff quarters, which occupied an old stable building.

She came to her feet and hovered there for a moment.

"Don't worry, dear," Meg answered her unspoken question. "Mum's the word."

CHAPTER 13

When Isolde stepped out onto the terrace, the wind was bracing. The skies were partially covered by gathering rainclouds, and most of the guests had taken themselves indoors in anticipation of a deluge. After a quick survey of the area, she spotted Tristan, who was seated on one of the garden benches arranged along the back wall of the terrace, where a single pocket of sun still shone, and seemed so lost in thought as to be oblivious to the gathering storm.

As she started towards him, she spotted something unusual.

At first, it appeared to be falling rain, silhouetted against a shaft of sunlight. However, no rain was falling, so she knew it couldn't be that.

Sand?

Dust?

Her eyes followed the shimmering trail upward, tracing it all the way to the rooftop above, which was edged with stone crenelations as an architectural homage to the castle nearby.

Her breath caught in her throat.

One of the heavy pieces of stone had come loose, scattering dust particles to the ground below, and was teetering on the very edge, liable to fall at any second. Tristan was seated directly beneath the parapet, and would undoubtedly be hit.

Before the thought had fully formed in her mind, she was running, calling out to him as she sprinted from one end of the terrace to the other.

"*Tristan*!"

He looked up in surprise, but had no time to speak before she'd taken his arm in a vice-like grip and yanked him out of his seat, the force of her energy pulling them both to the ground.

Seconds later, the stone fell, crushing the wooden bench where he'd been sitting with a *thud*.

A bit shaken, they picked themselves up and looked down at the wreckage.

"The stone," Isolde said, still breathing hard. "I saw it was about to fall. You would have been hit."

He nodded, and pulled her into his arms. "A life for a life," he said, his voice muffled against her hair. "Thank you."

"There's no need to thank me."

He rested his forehead against hers. "In case of any doubt, I want you to know this isn't projection," he said, to make her laugh. "Although, I don't think my heart can take too many more of these brushes with Mother Nature."

"Do you think the wind dislodged the stone?" she asked him. "It's been strong, the past couple of days."

"I think it's worth checking," he said. "Come on."

They went back inside to find a small group of residents had gathered, having heard the crash.

"Nothing to worry about, folks," Tristan said. "Just a little accident, and no harm done."

His uncle rushed from the manager's office to see what had caused the commotion.

"Are you all right?" Mark said, looking between the pair of them. "What on Earth happened?"

"One of the stone crenelations fell," Tristan explained, in an undertone so as not to cause any panic. "I need to get up onto the roof and check there aren't any others coming loose—didn't we have the roofers check the whole area before opening?"

Mark nodded. "Yes, they went over everything," he said. "Mind you, it's been one storm after another, lately, and being on the headland means we'll always bear the brunt of it."

"I'll take a look, anyway," Tristan said.

"Do you want company?" Mark asked.

Tristan nodded. "All right," he said. "I'll meet you up there in a few minutes."

First, he wanted to reassure his mother, who'd seen Isolde streaking across the terrace and been stricken with worry.

"That was a close call," one of the other guests said, and gave him a friendly clap on the back. "You were lucky there!"

Tristan frowned, because it occurred to him that the odds of that particular stone coming loose exactly when he happened to be seated beneath it were probably very long indeed.

It was something to think about.

Tristan joined his uncle on the crenelated portion of the roof, which was accessed via a spiral stone staircase on the southernmost corner of the house. Its design was vaguely mediaeval, in homage to the area, but the construction was more modern, having been built in the 1700s.

"Can you see anything?"

Mark looked up from his inspection of the missing stone. "It looks to be as we thought," he said, coming to his feet again. "The mortar looks a bit crumbly around where the stone used to sit, so perhaps the roofers didn't check everything they should have."

Tristan crossed the leaded roof and crouched down beside the stonework, as his uncle had done. He peered at the mortar, then at the surrounding stones, before sitting back on one knee.

"It's strange that the stones on either side seem completely solid," he said. "Whereas, as you say, the area around the missing stone looks crumbled."

He touched a hand to the dusty residue still sitting on the lead flashing.

"I'll call the roofers out again, first thing tomorrow," Mark said. "They were paid to do a proper job—"

Tristan rose to his feet, and began checking around the entire perimeter of the crenelations. He saw clearly where repair works had been done, here and there, and stopped to apply gentle pressure to some of the stones as he made his way around. It took several minutes to cover the distance, and when he returned his face was unreadable.

"I can't find any other loose stones," he said. "Just that one."

He thought again of the probabilities, and decided that the odds had just lengthened even more than before.

"It's cold up here," Mark said. "Come on, son. Let's go back inside, and put the whole thing from your mind. I'll have a stonemason come out and replace or repair that stone, as soon as possible."

Tristan looked at the gap in the stonework one last time, and then rose to his feet.

"Book them in first thing, Monday morning," he said. "There's another storm coming tonight, so there could be further damage by tomorrow."

He only hoped it was stonework, and nothing more.

Tristan returned to the library, where he found his mother seated beside Isolde, who'd been doing her best to reassure Meg that all would be well. He would recall that act of kindness later, but, for now, he added it to a growing list of things to admire.

"Well?" she asked him. "What did you find up there?"

Tristan leaned down to kiss his mother's cheek.

"Nothing of interest," he said, coming to sit beside Isolde. "It's possible the roofers didn't pick up on some loose mortar, and that's why the stone came away in the wind."

"I'm so glad Isolde was there to pull you to safety," Meg said, in a shaking voice.

Tristan took both of her hands in his. "Don't think about what might have been," he said. "I'm here now, and I'm safe."

Meg nodded. "I just don't know what I'd do, if—"

"I'm not going anywhere," he soothed her. "It'd take more than a knock on the head to see me off, anyway."

Meg's lips twitched. "Rely on you to make a bad joke, at a time like this."

"You can rely on me to make a bad joke at *any* time," he said, and teased another smile from her.

"Oh, all right," she said. "That's enough handwringing from me. Look at the time! Go on, the pair of you, and get ready for the auction. The place is heaving with guests, and I've already seen people coming downstairs in their frocks. It's black tie, and I won't have you shaming me, Tristan Alexander Williams."

Isolde grinned at the full use of his name.

"I'll come and find you again in half an hour, and I promise I'll wear a clean shirt," he said. "Do you need anything?"

"I'll be just fine," Meg said, but cast a wary eye outside the window, where the wind had picked up even more than before and sent a few of the garden chairs tumbling onto their backs. "It doesn't look too good out there, now. The sky looks ready to break."

They followed the direction of her gaze and had to agree; the clouds looked ominous.

"Let's put a few more lights on, around here," Tristan said. "That'll brighten the place up."

He moved off and began turning on the side lights. Left alone for a minute or two, Meg reached across to take Isolde by the hand.

"Thank you," she said. "I don't know what I would have done if I'd lost him."

Isolde shook her head. "There's no need to thank me," she mumbled. "Anybody would have done the same thing."

"I'm not sure about that. Some people seem to freeze up in moments of crisis, but not you. You're strong, like he is."

Was she strong? Isolde wondered.

She hadn't felt strong, out there on the terrace. The aches and pains she'd had over the past few weeks paled by comparison to the raw, visceral fear she'd felt when she'd seen the loose stone on the parapet, and the prospect of being too late to save him.

She asked herself whether the feeling would have been the same, had it been any other hotel guest sitting out there on the bench. Would she have experienced the same urgency? Would she have been so moved to reach them in time? Although she liked to think so, the small, honest voice at the back of her mind said otherwise.

"That's better," Tristan said, on his return. "We'd better get going, if I'm going to scrub up to my mother's approval."

He gave Meg a kiss, and then turned to Isolde.

"Shall we?"

CHAPTER 14

When Tristan and Isolde emerged from the library, it was to find a stream of guests had arrived at the hotel from all parts of the county, many of whom would be staying overnight. Staff whisked suitcases back and forth from the reception area and Mark had come into his own, chatting easily with the guests while making light of the weather, which was looking more torrential with every passing minute.

"Mr Williams?"

Tristan turned to find the bar manager waiting to speak to him.

"Yes, what is it, Simon?"

"I'm sorry to disturb you, sir, but I wonder if I could have a word in private?"

Tristan frowned, and turned back to Isolde. "I'll see you at dinner," he said, and she nodded, curious as to what had brought on the shift in his mood. She put it out of her mind, telling herself it was probably some staffing or supply issue, and hurried upstairs to change in time for the event.

She took the time to call Maeve, hoping to find her friend was free for a quick chat, but there was no answer. Resolving to try again later, she threw herself in the shower and sang the entire back catalogue of *Singin' in the Rain* at the top of her lungs while she scrubbed off the day.

By the time she made her way down to the ballroom shortly before six o'clock, the room was already full, but there was no sign of Tristan.

"Isolde!"

She spotted Gabi, who stood beside Luke as they welcomed their guests and guided them to one of ten large, circular tables. The room itself was beautiful; not too big nor too small, but perfectly proportioned. Plasterwork mouldings decorated the walls and four large chandeliers hung from the ceiling, which lent a nostalgic air to the proceedings and spoke of grandeur from another time. At the head of the room, a small stage had been erected in front of a large projector screen, while a space had been left clear in front of it for dancing, later. A series of large oil and watercolour paintings had been hung especially for the occasion from a brass picture rail running around the perimeter of the room, thereby allowing guests to see what was on offer.

Isolde side-stepped a woman in a long green dress and pearls to join Gabi beside a large board displaying a printed table plan.

"Looks like a good turnout, despite the weather," she said. "Luke must be pleased."

"There were a few last-minute cancellations, but that's always to be expected," Gabi replied. "Considering it's blowing a gale out there, we've done really well."

"Is Tristan around?"

Gabi forgot the other guests and swung around to face her. "Now, why would you be asking me *that*, I wonder?"

Isolde lifted a shoulder. "He's growing on me."

"I knew you two would hit it off!"

"It's just our names, and the circumstances…" she said. "It isn't *real*."

"I agree that it was probably a million-to-one shot that you'd be rescued by a man whose name matches yours—or, to put it another way, that you would happen to meet another person whose parents liked the old legend just as much as yours did. That doesn't mean your attraction for one another isn't real."

Isolde supposed that was true, but…

"I barely know him. Doesn't that seem *crazy*?"

"Well, if it is, it runs in the family," Gabi said, and looked across at her husband, who was shaking hands with the local mayor. "Luke and I hit things off pretty quickly, and you know I was engaged previously so I know all about long term versus short term relationships. All I can tell you from my own experience is that, sometimes, you can be with the wrong person for years, and the right person for no time at all."

Her words echoed the advice Meg had given her that very afternoon. "Have you been conferring with his mother?"

"What?"

"Never mind," she muttered. "Do you need any help?"

"No, I'm stuck here until everyone is seated, but why don't you go and sit down at the table and we'll join you when we can? Luke will mostly be on stage compering, but you and I are on the same table with the others."

Isolde made her way through the crowd to Table 1, on the edge of the dance floor. Music played in the background, something light and serene to help drown out the sound of the wind and rain that battered the windows on all sides, while servers moved around the room bearing trays of champagne.

Sophie, Gabriel, Nick and Kate were already seated, and two place settings remained free for Luke and Gabi, leaving one for her and another three for Meg, Tristan and Mark Williams. A quick glance at the place cards told her that some Good Samaritan, mostly likely Gabi, had seated her beside Tristan.

"Cupid strikes again," she murmured, and then smiled at her fellow diners. "How was your day?"

"Mine was great," Kate said. "I spent most of the morning in bed, because this is one of the rare occasions when we don't have a rumbunctious six-year-old waking us up at the crack of dawn. We had a lazy lunch and then a wander around the grounds and down to the beach. The day just flew by."

"Well, I wish I could say I had a lie-in," Sophie said, and gave her fiancé the side-eye. "*This* one woke up at silly o'clock to work on his latest novel, and was about as quiet as a bull in a china shop. He doesn't even have the excuse of being a six-year-old."

Gabriel laughed, and held up his hands. "I admit, I *might* have been a bit noisy on the keyboard," he said. "But, when inspiration strikes, you have to go with it."

"It's true, you have to go where the muse takes you," Nick said, in solidarity.

"Working odd hours and being led by inspiration must be the same in all creative professions," Isolde said. "What's it like working in the police, Sophie? Do you need to be creative when you're solving crimes?"

The newly appointed Detective Inspector Sophie Keane hadn't really thought of her work in that way before, but Isolde had a point. There *was* some creativity involved in problem solving, piecing together facts, dealing with difficult witnesses, and—

"There's a lot of creative swearing, that's for sure."

Isolde laughed, but any further discussion was interrupted by Tristan's arrival, alongside Mark and Meg. He made sure his mother was comfortable at the table before turning to the others gathered there.

"Good evening," he said to the assembly. "Hello, Isolde."

He came to sit beside her, with his mother on his other side happily chatting to Sophie about all things to do with crime and punishment in the county of Cornwall.

"You look beautiful," he said quietly, taking in the sapphire blue satin. "The colour matches your eyes."

"Thanks, you're not so bad yourself," she said, appreciating the black tuxedo he wore with panache.

He leaned in, resting his arm along the back of her chair so that only she would hear him.

"I was hoping you'd dance with me, later."

"I could probably manage that," she said. "Unless you've got two left feet. That would spoil the illusion I have of you, at the moment."

"What illusion is that?"

"Oh, you know. Brave, strong, handsome type who runs around saving helpless women before breakfast, that sort of thing."

"Actually, you're my first rescue," he said. "And, two things, just for the record."

She waited, while he took a sip of water.

"In the first place, you weren't helpless."

She inclined her head. "And, in the second place?"

"You should know that I never exert myself before breakfast—with one exception, of course"

"Which is?" she said, naively.

He smiled slowly, eyes full of promise, and she felt heat rush through her body.

"I think you'd at least need a bacon sandwich," she said.

He laughed richly, and would have said more, but there came a tap on the mic.

"If I could have your attention, please?" Luke said, from his position on the stage. He waited for conversation to die down, and for people to take their seats. "Welcome, everyone, to the charity auction this evening, and thank you very much for making the effort to travel on what's turned out to be a bit of a miserable night."

There were a few witters around the room.

"Before we get started, I'd like to thank our generous hosts, Tristan and Meg Williams, and, of course, Mark Williams, who manages this beautiful hotel," he said. "This evening wouldn't have been possible without them, so, if we could raise our glasses in a toast—"

The room followed his lead and came to their feet.

"To the Williams Family!" Luke called out, and the words were repeated around the ballroom.

Tristan raised a hand to wave, and then motioned that they should all sit down and be comfortable again.

"All right, folks, let's get things started. First up is Lot 1, a large oil painting of Mousehole village at dawn, by local artist Kate Williams. Do I have three hundred pounds? Three hundred! Yes, madam, on table three in the corner. Can anyone do better? Yes! Four hundred? I have four hundred..."

The bidding continued while Kate looked on in bemusement, unable to believe that people would pay so much for one of her paintings.

"I have two thousand five hundred pounds… going…going…gone! To the gentleman on table seven. Thank you, sir."

They all clapped, and congratulated Kate on having produced something so lovely, the proceeds of which would go to a wonderful cause. The auction continued, pausing occasionally to allow the kitchen to serve each of four courses and, between the second and third, Tristan took a turn around the room, greeting every guest with a smile and a handshake.

"Now that's done, I can relax," he said, reclaiming his seat next to Isolde. "Your lot is next, isn't it?"

She checked the little printed leaflet and nodded.

"So it is," she said.

As the waiter came around to replenish their glasses, Tristan stopped him and said something in his ear, to which the young man shook his head. Isolde had no intention of eavesdropping, but she heard the name 'Danielle', and remembered Tristan's discussion with her the previous night.

"Everything all right?" she asked.

Tristan drummed his fingers on the tabletop. "It's one of our staff," he said. "A girl called Danielle—"

Before he could continue, Luke tapped the mic again, and called for hush around the room so that the auction could continue. Intrigued by what Tristan had been about to say, Isolde was surprised when a picture of herself popped up on the projector screen, a professional shot in black and white that was often used in press calls and interviews which Luke had obviously obtained from somewhere online. Beneath it was detailed the mentoring sessions she'd offered, and bidding was opened up to the room.

"Lot thirty-seven is close to my heart, since it's been donated by my sister, Isolde," Luke said. "She's a world class journalist and public relations expert, and has very kindly offered a number of mentoring sessions to one lucky bidder. Now, who'll give me two hundred, to get the ball rolling?"

To her surprise, Isolde watched several hands fly into the air.

"Two hundred, I'm bid. Three? Three hundred?"

A man at the next table along craned his neck across to where she was seated and decided he could use some mentoring, after all.

"Five hundred," he called out.

"Thank you, sir, five hundred I'm bid—"

"I never thought it would be this popular," Isolde whispered in Tristan's ear. "I think—"

"One thousand."

Tristan spoke the words clearly, and she almost dropped the spoon she was holding.

"You don't need to bid for this," she muttered. "You can have all the mentoring you like!"

"I'll hold you to that," he said. "But this is all in a good cause, isn't it?"

He cast an eye towards the other man, who took up the unspoken challenge and upped his bid again.

"One thousand five hundred!"

The bidding went back and forth between them until, apparently, Tristan's opponent realised it was a battle he was unlikely to win.

A lot of money later, and Isolde was wondering what in the world she could possibly teach Tristan Williams about drumming up good PR, considering he'd managed to set tongues wagging and cameras snapping in one masterful swoop already.

"That should help the RNLI, shouldn't it?" he said.

She wasn't fooled for a minute. "Don't you think that was a bit steep?"

"If anything, it's far less than your time is worth."

She folded her arms over her chest, and waited.

"All right," he admitted. "*And* I couldn't stand the thought of Tim Judd getting to spend hours on end in your company, drooling."

She was shocked. "You...you were *jealous*?"

"Is that such a surprise? I'm as human as the next guy."

"Yes, I know, but...well, you just don't look the type to ever feel jealous."

He laughed. "What 'type' is that? And, please, don't say 'forgettable'."

"Har, har. *No*, you have everything going for you," she said. "Why would you need to feel jealous?"

"Nobody *needs* to feel it," he said. "If you must know, I'm as surprised as you are. I can't remember the last time I felt jealous of anyone or anything, but it seems you bring out the worst in me, as well as the best."

She didn't know what to make of that, but it was honest, which was a quality she valued highly.

He leaned forward, intending to say something else, when there came another tap on the mic.

"I thought the auction had finished," Sophie remarked, across the table.

"Yes, so did I," Gabi said, and wondered why Luke had taken to the stage again. Next on the schedule for the evening was an hour or two of dancing, and he'd already made his parting remarks.

"Ladies and gentlemen, I'm sorry to interrupt your dinner, once again. I'm afraid I've just been informed that the storm has caused severe flooding over the past few hours, and there's a risk that the road will be closed very soon. It's therefore with regret that I must ask those of you who aren't staying overnight in the hotel to gather your belongings; a free bus service has been arranged and is waiting outside. If you have any questions, please ask me, or one of the hotel staff."

A cacophony rose up at the end of his statement, with at least two thirds of the gathered assembly hurrying to leave the ballroom, as if it had just been announced that Noah was about to leave with his ark.

"Nick—" Kate began.

"I know, I was thinking the same thing," he said, and turned to their friends. "We'd planned to stay overnight, but if there's a risk of flooding carrying over into tomorrow, that'll be difficult because we need to get home to pick up Jamie."

"It's best if you two get on the bus, then," Gabi suggested. "We can have your luggage sent on, or Luke and I will drop it off on our way home, if that's any help?"

"That would be brilliant, thanks," Nick said, and the pair of them came to their feet. They made some hasty farewells and were about to hurry off to join the bus queue, when Kate paused and turned back to Isolde. "It was lovely to meet you—I hope to see you again, soon."

"You too," Isolde replied, and was touched that she'd bothered to stop, when they were clearly in a rush.

A short while later, Tristan returned to the table, having left to ensure the safe departure of the coach, which had now taken the majority of the evening's crowd. It left the ballroom feeling bare, a little like Miss Haversham's dining room, with plates piled high with uneaten profiteroles and half-drunk cups of coffee.

"It's bleak out there," he said, reaching for his coffee. "The rain is coming down in sheets."

His hair was slick with it, as was his tuxedo jacket, which he took off and hung on the back of his chair. Then, he turned to his mother.

"I think it would be best if you stayed in the hotel tonight," he suggested. "Mark's having a room prepared now."

Meg nodded. "I'd much rather be safe and warm here in the hotel, on a night like th—"

She was interrupted by the sound of an enormous crash outside, so loud as to shake the foundations of the house.

Seconds later, the room was plunged into darkness.

CHAPTER 15

A scream went up amongst the remaining crowd, whose faces were illuminated only by the candelabra that burned on the centre of each table. There followed an unnatural silence, broken only by the continuing howl of the wind outside.

Tristan came to his feet and raised his voice so that he could be heard.

"Ladies and gentlemen, the storm must have taken down one of the power lines, but we have plenty of candles and torches here, as well as comfortable rooms to see us all through the night, so there's absolutely no need to worry."

He signalled to one of the staff.

"Now, what I suggest is that those of you who already have a room with us go back there now for your own comfort and safety," he said. "I can see that our staff are already lighting more candles and they will be happy to guide you to your individual rooms to avoid any mishaps. For any remaining guests who don't have a room with us, and weren't able to leave on the bus, we will be happy to provide accommodation. For now, stay at your tables and our staff will come to each of you in turn. Please, don't wander off into the darkness without one of us with you; this is a very old house and there are a lot of hazards, so we'd like to avoid any accidents."

There were a few questions, which he fielded easily, and then Mark reappeared with several staff bearing torches. He left them to direct the guests safely to their rooms, then hurried back over to their table, the white light of his torch shaking slightly with the tremble of his hand.

"I had a look outside," he said to Tristan, in an undertone. "One of the biggest trees has come down on the driveway, blocking it completely. It's taken the power line with it."

Tristan gripped the edge of his chair. "What about the emergency generator?" he asked, keeping his voice low. "Why hasn't that kicked in, yet?"

"It doesn't seem to be working—"

"The place is going to get very cold, very quickly," Tristan said. "Tell the remaining staff to go around every room with extra blankets and food provisions, and instruct the guests to remain in their rooms unless there's an emergency, in which case they should come back here."

Mark nodded.

"After that's done, tell the staff to stay in here so there's always someone around," he said. "Besides, it's safer and drier than having to brave the weather outside to get back to their own quarters."

After that, he left briefly to go in search of one of the younger female staff, and returned with her in tow.

"Mum? Ellie is going to take you to your room now, and stay with you for as long as you like," he said. "I don't want you to feel lonely in the darkness, or have any trouble manoeuvring around if you need to. I'll come and see you as soon as I can."

"Do whatever you need to do, and don't worry about me—Ellie and I will get along just fine," Meg said, and patted his cheek before turning to Isolde. "Look after each other—and be careful."

With which prescient words, she left.

Tristan took out his mobile phone, only to find there was no signal and no internet connection.

"Damn," he muttered, and slipped the phone back into his pocket. "Does anybody else have a signal?"

One by one, their heads began to shake.

"Nothing," Isolde said.

"Nothing here, either," Luke said, and came to his feet. "Tell us what we can do to help?"

Tristan ran an agitated hand through his hair, then let it fall away again.

"I'm worried about one of our staff, a young woman called Danielle Teague," he said. "I'm concerned she may be missing."

Sophie leaned forward, all business now. "Why do you say 'missing'?"

"She was supposed to be at work this morning," Tristan said. "She never turned up."

"She's probably sitting at home, or at some other hotel," Mark put in. "You know what I said about these seasonal staff—"

"She *isn't* at home," Tristan said quietly. "I rang her home address and spoke to her parents this afternoon. They told me they haven't heard from her at all, and haven't seen her. The staff haven't seen her since the end of her shift, last night."

"Has anyone checked her room?" Sophie asked. "Are her things still there?"

"I went over earlier today to knock on the door, but nobody answered," Tristan said. "I let myself in with the master key and it looked to me as though her things are all still there, which is why I'm worried. I rang the local police, who said to give it another few hours before making a report, but with the power outage and this storm…I would hate to think she's out there somewhere, in need of help."

Isolde listened, and understood now why he'd been so distracted.

"If there's any danger at all of her being missing on site here, then we should arrange a search party," Sophie said. "I'd suggest starting with her room again, in case she's gone back there since you last checked, followed by a full search of the staff quarters—"

"I don't mind heading over," Mark volunteered.

"I'll check the tunnel and any unoccupied guest bedrooms," Tristan offered.

"I'll come with you," Isolde said, but he shook his head.

"The tunnel's dangerous at the best of times," he said. "I couldn't risk you going down there in a long dress, or have you falling over in the dark. I think it would be safest if you, Gabi and Sophie—"

"No offence, champ, but if you're about to tell us little women to sit around here and wait, then you've got another thing coming," Sophie said, coming to her feet and nudging him firmly aside. "Isolde, Gabi, Tristan does have a point; you're both in long dresses, so why don't you head back to your rooms to change into something more practical, then go and start with the attics and work your way down? We have to work methodically."

They agreed.

"Good," Sophie said. "I'm already in trousers, so I'll kick off my heels before heading down to search the cliff trails and Haven beach, with Gabriel."

Her fiancé barely held back a groan, having already anticipated he'd be roped into one of the less salubrious tasks.

The things you did for love...

"Luke, head over to the outbuildings, in case she's in there."

Now it was settled, Sophie looked around each of them in turn, their faces appearing like ghostly effigies in the dying candlelight.

"Reconvene here when you're finished—does everyone have access to a clock and a torch?"

Their phones might not have had any useful signal, but they could still tell the time, and Mark had procured enough torches for each pair in the search party.

"All right," Sophie said. "Let's keep this quick and efficient, so panic doesn't spread amongst the other guests. Whether you've finished searching your area or not, be back here in an hour. Agreed?"

They agreed and, with one last, parting look, Tristan and Isolde went their separate ways.

CHAPTER 16

Mark stopped by the Manager's Office to collect the long, waterproof overcoat he kept hanging on a peg on the back of the door, covered himself as best he could, and then swapped his smart black dress shoes for the pair of hiking boots he kept handy for occasions such as these. Then, he grabbed up his torch and a large set of keys, pulled the hood over his head and made for the terrace doors on the other side of the reception hall, which gave swiftest access to the staff quarters on the far side of the terrace and formal gardens.

He took a deep breath and unbolted the lock, clinging onto the edge of the wood as the wind blew the door wide open, rushing into the hallway and nearly taking him off his feet. He planted one foot in front of the other and stepped outside, pulling the door shut behind him. It blew open again twice, but on the third attempt he managed to keep it closed and quickly locked it again from the outside, fumbling the keys with one hand while the other clung on to the handle for dear life. His hood blew off and, within seconds, Mark was drenched, the rain driving in from all directions and at speed, rocking him on his feet and running down the gap in his coat.

He set his shoulders, pulled the torch from his pocket and made his way through the wind, heading for the northern edge of the formal gardens, beyond which there was the former stable block hidden neatly behind some tall hedging. It was accessible via the main driveway at the front of the hotel, but also via a pedestrian gate with a coded lock known only by hotel staff, allowing them to come and go more easily and enter the hotel via one of several back doors, including the kitchen.

Mark made it to the gate, though his eyes were blurry with rainwater and his coat stuck to his knees, which made movement even more difficult. Breathing hard, he shone the torch light on the locking mechanism, entered the key code and pushed through, slamming the gate behind him. Then, he hurried the short distance towards the outer door of the staff quarters, which required a key to enter. He shook out the selection of keys he held in his cold hand, blinking as water ran in rivulets down his face, before finding the one he needed, shoving it in the lock and practically falling inside.

The small foyer of the old stables was bizarrely quiet after such an onslaught, and Mark stood there in the darkness for a moment, torch light trained on the ground as he caught his breath. Water collected in a puddle at his feet, then squelched as he turned around and made his way towards one of two doors: one to his left, on the ground floor, which led along a long passageway spanning the length of the stables and housing five en-suite staff bedrooms; and another door directly ahead of him, which led upstairs and to a mirror-image passageway, housing a further five bedrooms.

Mark started forward, feet squelching against the tiled floor, and caught a movement in his peripheral vision. He spun around, torch bobbing in his hand, and saw a tall shadow of a man in the mirror dead ahead.

He expelled a long breath, laughed at his own foolishness, and crossed the small lobby to open the door leading upstairs. Having recently checked the records, he knew that Danielle Teague occupied room number 7 on the first floor of the block, so that was the most logical place to start.

Mark's footsteps creaked on the old wooden stairs, his hand gripping the banister rail as he moved upward to the landing at the top. His torch guided him through the penetrating darkness, passing doors with numbers painted in black until he came to one bearing the number '7'.

He paused, listening for signs of life beyond it, or from the doors on either side, and then raised his fist to knock.

No answer.

He tried again, louder this time.

Still, no answer.

Mark took out his keychain once again and retrieved the master key, which he used to let himself inside Danielle's room. He stood in the doorway and shone his torchlight into all four corners, noting the unmade bed and haphazard piles of clothing and other detritus discarded on the floor, but definitely no sign of life.

He stepped inside, and began to search for anything helpful.

His eye passed over a collection of pictures and magazine cuttings fixed to the wall, all featuring images of exotic foreign countries, and then fell on a little wooden desk. There was nothing much there, only a few receipts and some nail polishes in the drawer, but no papers, stationery or books. He moved onto the wardrobe, pulling it open to reveal a small selection of work and casual clothes, a couple of dresses and a few pairs of shoes, all well-worn apart from a couple of new pairs of very expensive heels. He poked around at the back but found nothing of interest, then moved onto the bed, crouching down to peer beneath it, shining his torch this way and that.

Standing up again, Mark turned to the only other piece of furniture in the room, which was a chest of drawers. He rummaged through them, pushing aside underwear and socks, t-shirts and pyjamas, but found nothing.

He turned to leave, the torchlight projecting a wide arc of light against the back wall, and glanced at the magazine cut-outs again. When he looked more closely, he found there was one image that didn't match the rest. It was a real photograph—a rarity in the digital age—printed and worn, featuring a slightly younger Danielle standing beside an older man, somewhere in his early thirties. He held his arm around her and both of them were smiling.

The man in the picture was his nephew, Tristan.

Mark reached out a hand and tugged it from the wall, looked at it again to be sure his eyes hadn't deceived him, and then slid the photograph into his pocket for safekeeping.

"I distinctly recall you saying that you'd be 'off duty' this weekend," Gabriel said, and moved the torch so that Sophie could see better. "In fact, you told everyone the same thing, only last night."

Sophie paused in the act of tugging on a pair of walking shoes.

"*When inspiration strikes,*" she crooned. "You said so yourself. Mysteries and missing people are my muse, that's all."

Gabriel rolled his eyes, and had to admit he'd asked for that one. "You can't *really* think the girl's out there, somewhere?" he persisted. "Sophie, the Met Office has issued a severe weather warning telling people not to venture outside unnecessarily. That includes you."

"This *is* necessary," she argued. "What if Danielle's lying out there, injured?"

He sighed. "All right," he said, and cursed his own decency. "Where do you want to start?"

"We'll make for the clifftop path," she said, and almost laughed at his expression, which was a comical mask of horror.

"Sophie, that's the last place we should go. Gusts of wind and sheer drops don't go well together."

"I'll hold your hand," she said.

Gabriel had to smile. "I suppose I always knew that life with you would never be dull," he said.

"You wouldn't want it any other way," she replied, and reached up to plant a kiss on his mouth. "Now, come on. We've got a young woman to find."

"Yes, ma'am."

CHAPTER 17

Gabi and Isolde hurried back to their rooms to change into more casual clothing. Having only one torch between them, it meant taking each of their rooms in turn, but they moved swiftly and were both ready to go within the space of five minutes.

"Do you know how to get up to the attics from here?" Isolde asked, shining the torch either way along the corridor.

"No, we'll have to look around," Gabi said. "It's highly unlikely Danielle would have found her way up there and become trapped, but we have to be thorough and check anyway. Sophie's told me about cases where she'd find something, or someone, in a place that was totally unexpected, but there was always an explanation once all of the facts were pieced together."

"It's the same with journalism," Isolde said, deciding to turn left along the corridor and try their luck in that direction. "You fit the pieces together to build the story. I'm worried about this girl, Gabi. If her things are still in her room, and her parents haven't heard from her—"

"I'm worried, too," her sister-in-law replied. "I hate to think anything might have happened to her."

They fell silent, imagining the fear of being caught in the darkness, or, worse yet, the storm outside.

"Look, there's a staircase here," Isolde said, and shone the torch towards what appeared to be an old servant's staircase.

"That leads to some of the smaller bedrooms on the next floor up," Gabi said. "But let's follow it and see if there's another level after that."

They climbed the stairs as quickly as they could, their footsteps sounding impossibly loud in the surrounding darkness. Reaching the upper landing, they paused again to determine the best direction, and decided to keep to the northern end of the hotel, where a door marked 'PRIVATE' restricted access to guests.

"This looks like the housekeeping corridor," Isolde said, and tugged the door open. "Let's try this way."

They wandered along a short corridor with doors on either side, until they spotted a quaint little staircase in miniature.

"Up there," Gabi said. "It looks as though that staircase leads to a higher level."

Isolde trained the light in that direction, and they followed it upward through another closed door. The carpet ended on the threshold and was replaced with bare wooden treads that protested beneath their weight and caused both women to stop dead in their tracks.

"D' you reckon anybody ever comes up here?" Isolde whispered, while her hand gripped the edge of an ancient banister.

"Not likely," Gabi grumbled, clutching the wall for support. "Why are you whispering, anyway?"

"It's a bad habit," Isolde replied, and thought immediately of her walk through the cave with Tristan.

"You know what I need, after this?" Gabi said, as they started upstairs again.

"What's that?"

"A nice, relaxing weekend away at a country house hotel."

Isolde couldn't help but laugh.

Downstairs, Sophie and Gabriel stood beside the terrace doors and tried to open them, without success.

"They aren't bolted, so they must have been locked from the outside," Gabriel said. "I can't see a key anywhere, can you?"

Sophie shone their torch over the whole door again, and shook her head.

"Nothing," she said. "Maybe one of the others had to lock it after they went outside, to keep the wind out."

"We'll have to go around the front and double back to pick up the cliff path," Gabriel said, and checked the time on his mobile phone. "We're already ten minutes into your hour, so we need to get moving if we're going to try and make it down to the beach."

Sophie grabbed his arm and steered him through the candlelit hallway towards the concierge desk, where there was a stand filled with leaflets, including one listing the tide times.

She held it up to one of the candles.

"We've got about an hour and a half before the tide comes in this evening, although it would be on its way before then," she said. "You're right—let's get a move on."

They headed for the main entrance, the door to which was made of heavy oak and featured a solid latch closure.

"We can't leave this on the latch because it'll fly open, but, if we don't, it'll close behind us. Is there a key?" Sophie said, acutely aware of every wasted minute that ticked by.

Gabriel pointed the torchlight towards the Manager's Office.

"Let's try in here, in case Mark keeps a set somewhere."

They ducked inside and scanned the walls for a key safe, but found none.

"The desk," she suggested, and crossed the room to begin rifling through the drawers, only to find them locked. "It's no use, I can't see any keys for the front door."

"Let's try something else," Gabriel suggested, and spied the large sash window. "This opens onto the driveway outside, so why don't we climb through and leave it unlocked for the return journey?"

Sophie turned the torch on him.

"What were you, a cat burglar in a past life?"

He held up both hands, in mock surrender.

"Just a student with a knack for losing their keys after a night at the Union, I swear," he said. "I had a friend who used to keep their window open for me on Friday nights, just in case."

Sophie laughed, and then eyed up the window.

"All right, let's do this. Hold my torch."

Sophie and Gabriel shimmied their way through the sash window and out into the icy night air, landing on the gravel driveway in an undignified heap. The wind roared all around them as the eye of the storm closed in upon the people of Tintagel, but they pushed themselves onward, edging around the southern side of the hotel and then rounding the corner, where the wind was at its strongest on the cliffside. Sophie paused to look back at the house, swinging the torchlight with her, but saw no friendly light shining in the windows, other than the very dim glow of what remained of the candles in the ballroom. She thought she saw another white torchlight across the terrace, but didn't stop to wonder which of their search party it belonged to. Instead, she pointed towards the coastal path, which was accessed directly from the hotel gardens.

"This way!" she shouted.

Gabriel took her hand and kept it tightly in his own as they followed the pathway, keeping as far back from the cliffs as they could. It was chilling, with the sound of the wind and the crashing of waves all around, and the grim prospect of death remaining a very real possibility should they venture too close to the edge. Sophie swept the torch back and forth as they moved, checking the ground for any sign of Danielle, but found none.

Finally, they reached the top of the beach steps, and prepared to descend.

"Are you ready?" Gabriel shouted.

"I was born ready!" she called back, and Gabriel grinned through the darkness, wondering how he'd ever lived such a dull and quiet life before.

He took a firm grip of the wooden rail, told himself he'd had a good life, and started down the stairs.

CHAPTER 18

Gabi and Isolde climbed the attic stairs and found themselves in a network of eaves, each one separated by a series of A-frames that held up the main roof of the hotel. The storm was thunderous as it fell upon the old slate, echoing like a steel drum as they stood there, trying to gauge the darkness and whether they were alone in it. Isolde shone the torchlight all around, to see whether the attic roof was high enough for them to stand upright, which it was, but only in the central areas.

"Watch your head," she said, as they began to move over the old floorboards.

The light skittered over dusty boxes and suitcases, broken furniture, and stacks of newspapers that were yellowed with age, but there was no sign of Danielle Teague.

"I mean, who keeps newspapers from the sixties, for goodness' sake?" Gabi burst out. "Next, we'll find a rocking chair moving all by itself, with the faint sound of a musical box playing and some old teddy bear that used to belong to 'Little Johnny', the kid who vanished back in 1857."

Isolde laughed, a bit nervously. "Don't forget the wardrobe full of dresses belonging to the lady of the house back in the eighteenth century—who was kept up here in the attics after she went mad, of course."

"Of course," Gabi agreed, and they continued forward, stepping over the wooden joists to move into the next section of the roof.

"You know, if this is all an elaborate charade, I'll kill you," Isolde threw over her shoulder. "You did say that you wanted to run a murder mystery weekend, after all."

"I said that in the *daylight*," Gabi muttered. "I've had second thoughts about it since the power cut, the storm, the missing woman, and the creepy attic."

Isolde chuckled. "I don't think there's anything here—"

"Wait," Gabi said, and grabbed her arm. "Listen to that."

They stood perfectly still.

"It's the rain," Isolde said.

"No," Gabi said. "I heard something else, I'm sure of it."

"That's probably just my heart, hammering in my chest."

"No, definitely something else. Just listen."

They waited in silence, straining their ears beyond the sound of rainfall and wind, then it came.

Scratch, scratch, scratch.

"There!" Gabi whispered. "Did you hear that?"

"Yes!"

They waited again.

Scratch, scratch, scratch.

It was impossible to say where the sound was coming from, except that it was somewhere in that section of the attic. Isolde raised the torch and began sweeping the light over the floorboards, finding more old boxes and broken paraphernalia, then moving the light higher up the walls until, finally, it reached the eaves of the roof.

Where it fell upon a colony of bats.

The breath lodged in their throats.

"It's okay," Isolde whispered. "Bats are friendly creatures."

"Yeah, but we've all seen the movies," Gabi whispered back. "They're going to fly at us, any second now."

She made a good point.

"You know, I think we've searched enough," Isolde said. "Let's leave the attics to the bats."

"Yes, I agree—"

They took two careful, creaking steps backward before they heard the first flutter of a wing, and then, suddenly, the bats were all around their heads, chirping and squeaking like mice, the brush of their furry bodies coming at them unseen in the darkness.

Luke found the terrace doors locked, as Sophie and Gabriel had, and came to the same conclusion about the latch on the main front door. However, instead of finding a window to clamber through, he made his way through the ground floor of the hotel towards the kitchen, where he knew there was a back door that led out into a service courtyard that connected to the main driveway. From that courtyard, staff could follow a short pathway to the former stables, or access the other garages and outbuildings.

The kitchen staff had evacuated to the ballroom along with the rest, but there was a lingering scent of cooked meat on the air following their recent dinner service which permeated the darkness—and made his stomach rumble, since he hadn't had much of an opportunity to eat during the auction.

Telling himself to stay focused, Luke walked between the stainless-steel units and then turned left towards a smaller utility space where he found the back door, which was locked. That particular access route had been used by a number of his own gallery staff earlier that day, given its easy proximity to the service car park in the courtyard outside, so he happened to know the code to open the door mechanism.

Or, at least, he thought he did.

Luke's finger hovered over the mechanical keypad, while he cursed his feeble memory.

"It was something obvious," he muttered to himself, and tried *1-2-3-4*.

That didn't work.

"Okay, come on," he said to himself. "Just think back to earlier in the day. Now, what was the code?"

He tried *0-0-0-0* but still, the door wouldn't budge.

He swore to the empty room, and gave it one last shot.

4-3-2-1.

The handle turned, and the mechanism clicked open.

It was then that Luke realised he'd forgotten to grab a coat, a fact which became increasingly worrisome as a powerful gust of wind buffeted against the door. He shone his torch around the utility room, which was larger than the average and had formerly been the butler's pantry. To his relief, a long peg rail brimmed with a selection of coats belonging to the kitchen staff.

He borrowed the nearest to hand, and prepared to brave the elements.

Luke felt the force of the wind from the moment he stepped outside, and his first coherent thought was that, perhaps—just *perhaps*—the weather reports weren't quite so exaggerated, after all.

Keeping his head down, he ran across the courtyard towards the nearest of the hotel's outbuildings, which happened to be a quadruple garage used to store chauffeur-driven courtesy cars. He found the outer doors locked, and the key code was not the same as that for the utility room door, so he abandoned it in favour of the next outbuilding, which was the laundry.

This time, the key code worked, and he pushed inside.

The coat he'd borrowed hadn't fulfilled its basic purpose, for he could feel the rain seeping through his clothes, but he shook himself off and shone his torch around the space. It was deceptively large, with bare stone walls and floors, a row of washing machines and tumble driers along one side and what looked to be industrial ironing equipment along the other, as well as a workbench for folding. None of the machines was operational, but he was *sure* he heard a banging sound. He shone the torch this way and that, and walked slowly along the row of machines, but found nothing untoward.

Convinced he was imagining things, Luke was about to head back outside when he spotted an internal door that would lead him through to the next outbuilding. Keen to avoid another soaking, he tugged it open, and immediately the sound of banging grew louder.

He stood in the doorway, his torch trained on the floor while he listened to the sound of rhythmic thuds coming from somewhere within. That part of the building was a storage facility, used to house chairs and tables for events such as the auction that evening, and was full of a hotchpotch of other furniture and boxes. He stepped inside and began to follow the banging sound, heart thumping in time as he moved through the darkness, and then—

He heard a moan, and it sounded like a woman in pain.

Luke followed the sound as quickly as he could, blood pounding in his ears, ready to face an attacker. He gripped the torch like a weapon, took a deep breath and rounded another stack of boxes to find—

To find a couple of the hotel staff enjoying themselves, on an old sofa.

They both let out a shriek of surprise, and raised their hands to block the torchlight that shone in their faces.

"Hey!"

Since Luke had experienced as much of a scare as they had, he wasn't feeling particularly forgiving.

"What the *hell* are you two doing out here?" he blazed.

"We were—"

"It was a rhetorical question," Luke said, holding up a hand. "It's blowing a hoolie out there, and you were told to stay in the ballroom!"

The young man, who couldn't have been more than nineteen in Luke's estimation, looked at the young woman beside him—who was not Danielle Teague—and then gave a very Gallic shrug.

"You've gotta take your chances, mate—"

"Listen, Casanova," Luke snapped. "We need everybody accounted for, so your extra-curricular activities will have to wait. Get back to the ballroom with everybody else—go on, move it!"

The pair of them scrambled up, hurried into their remaining clothes, and scuttled off like rats leaving a sinking ship.

In the wake of their departure, Luke smiled.

When you were young, you just didn't feel the cold.

CHAPTER 19

Gabi and Isolde clattered back down the attic stairs and into the main hotel once again, slamming the door shut behind them.

"Eugh!" Gabi said roundly, and threw her head upside down to shake out her hair. "I won't forget that experience in a hurry."

Isolde gave a whole-body shudder. "It was the *noise*," she said. "That scratching sound is going to haunt me."

"God only knows what's living in my hair, now," Gabi muttered. "Probably a family of spiders."

Isolde conducted a brief check.

"All clear," she pronounced. "Where to, next? Tristan is checking the unoccupied bedrooms, so I guess we should we go for the other main rooms in the hotel, followed by the basement?"

"Ah, *yes*," Gabi said. "To round off our *Little House of Horrors* experience for today, let's leave behind the bats in the attic and turn our attention to the mice in the basement."

Isolde laughed, and then checked the time.

"Actually, we won't have time to check everywhere, we're already coming up to fifty minutes since the start of the search."

"Okay," Gabi said. "Let's go downstairs and get around as much as we can."

They hurried back down to the ground floor using a set of service stairs and emerged beside the kitchen corridor.

"Let's start in there," Isolde said, and they stepped inside the kitchen.

"It's giving me *Jurassic Park* vibes," Gabi said, as they passed an enormous stainless-steel oven. "You know that scene, where the kids are hiding in the kitchen and the dinosaurs manage to open the door and start hunting them?"

"Yeah?"

"That."

Isolde snorted. "Luckily for you, dinosaurs have been extinc—"

She came to a shuddering stop, as a dark figure passed by the window straight ahead.

"Gabi—"

"I saw it, too."

Seconds later, a door handle turned somewhere in the room to their left, then a gush of wind whipped through the kitchen as the outer door opened. They waited with their hearts in their mouths, and heard the door shut again followed by the sound of heavy boots making their way inside—

"*Luke*!"

Both women spoke in unison, and he almost jumped out of his skin.

"For the love of God! What are you doing skulking around here?" he cried. "Are you trying to give me a heart attack?"

"We weren't skulking, we were *searching*," Isolde said, once her own heart rate had recovered. "There isn't much time before the hour is up, so we're going to head back to the ballroom shortly."

"I take it you didn't find anything in the attics?"

"Aside from a stack of newspapers and a load of bats? No, nothing," Gabi said. "How about you?"

"Nothing except a couple of randy teenagers," Luke said. "A couple of the serving staff had taken themselves off to one of the outbuildings for some "alone time" and I happened to walk in and disturb them."

"Their hormones must be raging," Isolde said. "You wouldn't catch me out there in a freezing cold barn on a night like this!"

"At the rate he was going, that kid probably didn't feel the cold," Luke was bound to say. "Come on, I could use a drink. Gabi, have you checked on Madge, lately?"

His wife nodded.

"She's fed, watered and walked as of an hour ago," she said. "She's got extra blankets in the meantime."

Luke was content with that, and wished that he, too, was fed, watered and tucked up in bed rather than scouring a large country house for a missing girl.

"Have you seen any of the others?" Isolde asked him, as they made their way back towards the ballroom.

Luke shook his head. "Nobody," he replied. "You?"

"No," Isolde said, and thought how strange it was that they hadn't bumped into Tristan as he was checking any of the spare hotel rooms.

Then she thought of the tunnel, and was worried.

When they entered the ballroom, which had been filled with people and laughter only an hour before, it was to find most of the staff gathered in a huddle or sleeping on the floor with blanket coverings, and their own table still empty.

"We're five minutes early, yet," Gabi reminded them.

Isolde nodded, but couldn't dispel a general feeling of disquiet.

Mark entered the room shortly afterwards, and stopped to have a word with the staff before heading over to join them.

"Hello again," he said. "No sign of the others?"

"Not yet," Luke replied. "Did you find anything interesting in Danielle's room, or in the staff quarters?"

"Possibly, but let's wait until we're all here," he said, in a strained voice. "My word, it's really shaking out there. I hope Sophie and Gabriel manage to get back up the cliff stairs all right, or we'll have to send out another search party."

DI Sophie Keane wasn't too proud to admit when she was wrong, and she was beginning to suspect she'd been dead wrong in suggesting that she and her fiancé head out into the storm to look for a young woman who was, as Mark had suggested, probably tucked up warmly in bed somewhere on the other side of the county. She thought this as they neared the bottom of the beach steps, after what had been a harrowing descent from the top of the cliffs, in pitch darkness, while being attacked by wind and rain from all sides.

When their feet touched sand at the bottom, she sent up a silent prayer of thanks.

"Which way first?" Gabriel called out, above the thundering waves.

"We haven't got long until the tide comes in!" Sophie called back. "Let's start from the northern end and work back towards Merlin's Cave and the castle. We can only check the beach, we'll have to leave the caves for tomorrow."

They set off along the sand, a single torchlight shining their way.

"What do we do if—" Gabriel started to ask her something, and then tumbled headlong into a fall, having tripped over something solid.

"*Gabe*—" Sophie rushed forward to help him, but he was already up and dusting himself off.

"Don't worry, I'm fine," he said, but took the torch from her hand to turn it back upon the sand, so that they could see clearly what had caused him to fall. "Sophie."

She had already seen it.

The body of a woman who had once been Danielle Teague lay in a crumpled heap on the sand, horribly bloated and barely recognisable except for her long hair and the hotel uniform she still wore. It was clear to Sophie's trained eye that the woman had been dead for some time in the water, but she held out a silent hand for the torch and moved forward to look more closely.

"She's been dead for quite a while," she said, once her stomach had ceased to roll. "It's hard to estimate these things, without a pathologist or forensic expert to hand, but experience tells me the body has been in the water for at least twenty-four hours."

Gabriel swallowed, and found his voice.

"That tallies with what Tristan told us about the staff not having seen her since yesterday evening."

Sophie nodded, and then, taking a pair of nitrile gloves from her pocket, she bent down to search the woman's pockets. Sure enough, she found a purse containing a single debit card with Danielle's name on it, which seemed to settle the matter.

"She matches the description, and her ID lines up," Sophie said, in a flat tone of voice. "It looks like I'll be launching an investigation here, after all."

"Murder?" he queried.

Sophie shone her torch over what looked to be an old head wound on the girl's skull, but knew from cases such as these that it was a hard matter to say whether it would have been sustained in or out of the water.

"Too early to say," she replied. "I'd classify this as a suspicious death, for now."

"What should we do?" Gabriel asked. "I mean, with her body?"

Sophie thought fast, with an eye for the rising tide.

"We can't risk her being washed out to sea again," she said, and glanced meaningfully towards the beach stairs.

Gabriel blew out a long breath, preparing himself for what was to come. "I'll put her over my shoulder," he said quietly. "Will that do?"

"We can wrap her in my coat," Sophie said. "I'll manage without."

"No, I'll be sweating like a pig on market day, anyway, by the time we reach the top of those steps," he said. "We'll wrap her in my coat, and then we'll burn it at a later date."

"Agreed. Gabe?"

"Yes?"

"Thank you for this. It's a dreadful task."

He nodded. "Yes, but she suffered a dreadful death, and her parents will want her home again."

Sophie put a hand on his arm. "Yes, they will."

CHAPTER 20

Tristan awakened to a mouthful of seawater.

He coughed, heaving the liquid from his lungs as he came back to full consciousness and a whole world of pain. The floor beneath him was hard and damp, providing no cushion for the deep head wound at the base of his skull, nor the sprained wrist he'd sustained when he'd fallen forward. His limbs felt shaky as he tried to rouse himself, but, before he could, another wash of seawater came at him, covering his whole body in an unexpected shock of cold water.

Completely wet through, he began to shiver, and reached out a hand to try to find purchase in the darkness, where the echo of the waves was deafening as the sea level continued to rise. He touched stone on either side, and his fingers gripped the rough edge of it as he pulled himself upward, fighting the dizzy feeling that he was going to collapse again.

He turned, feet sloshing in water that was now to his ankles, and felt his way blindly until he touched something that felt like old, rusted metal.

He knew where he was, then.

Williams Cave.

The last thing he remembered was entering the tunnel, and making his way down it with his torch in hand.

He never heard the footsteps approaching him from behind; the sound of the waves had been too loud, and whoever it was had needed no torch to light their way, for he'd provided a beacon for them to follow.

He never saw their face, nor heard their voice.

He only felt the force of blunt impact on the back of his head, and then nothing after then.

His hands gripped the iron bars of the gate, their peeling rust scraping the underside of his hands as he tried to open it, but it wouldn't move.

It had been locked, when he'd arrived.

When he'd reached the end of the tunnel, the gate was closed and locked, barring further entry to the cave beyond and he hadn't found the old iron key that would open it. Now, he found himself on the wrong side, which could mean only one thing: the same person who'd knocked him out had also unlocked it, dragged his inert body to the other side and then re-locked it again so that he couldn't return to safety.

The peril of his situation hit him like a blow to the chest, and he began shouting, calling out for somebody—anybody—to come and help, but his voice was swallowed by the sea that crashed in almighty waves against the cave walls.

He turned from the gate and felt the water lap against his shins.

There was no way to escape through the tunnel; that way was barred to him. If he did nothing, he would drown.

There was only one way out, and that was to swim for it.

He knew the shape of the cave roughly, and called it to mind from earlier in the day when he'd been in the same place walking hand in hand with Isolde.

Isolde.

He loved her.

It didn't seem possible, after so short a space of time, but he was a man who knew his own mind. He'd met some lovely women over the years, and had been privileged to call himself their friend and, in some cases, more than a friend. He'd loved them with care and kindness, but had never felt a tenth of the emotion he now felt for a woman he'd met only the day before.

Isolde would tell him he was foolish, and that it wasn't possible to feel that depth of emotion without coming to properly know a person. He'd simply tell her that he was starting from a higher point than most, and would look forward to falling even more in love with the woman he came to know.

It was an argument he was looking forward to having, and the prospect of it gave him something to live for.

He bent down, gritting his teeth against the pain, and undid the laces on his shoes before kicking them off. Next, he took off his soaked shirt and trousers, knowing they would only hold him back. He stood there in the shallows of the tunnel and stared through the darkness, picturing the layout of the cave before edging into the freezing water.

Thoughts of family and home, of work and friends and of the life he had yet to live all crowded into his mind in those dark moments where his future hung in the balance.

Then, he took a deep breath and dived in.

By the time the clock struck twenty minutes past the hour, Isolde was really starting to worry. Sophie, Gabriel and Tristan still hadn't returned, and it was no coincidence in her mind that theirs had been the most difficult areas to search.

"If they're not back in another five minutes, I think we should split up and look for them," she said.

Luke nodded. "Agreed. I know Sophie, and she's the kind of person to keep to the letter of a plan. If she and Gabe aren't back, it's because something's happened."

"What about Tristan?"

"I don't know him as well as I know the other two, but I'm surprised he isn't back yet."

Before they could debate the matter further, Sophie and Gabriel re-entered the ballroom looking harrowed. They'd taken the time to change their clothes, the reason for which would become clear to all of them soon enough, but there was no sign of Tristan.

The look on Sophie's face told them all clearly that she did not bear glad tidings.

"Is everybody here?" she asked, and ran a quick head count. "Where's Tristan?"

"We don't know," Isolde said, working hard to keep the worry from her voice. "Should we go and look for him?"

"Let's give him a few more minutes," Sophie said, and then, keeping her voice low so that it wouldn't carry, she imparted the news that couldn't be withheld any longer. "I'm sorry to say, we found the body of Danielle Teague down on Haven beach."

There was a stunned silence, and then Gabi let out a sob. "She's—she's dead?"

"Yes, and has been for at least a day," Sophie replied. "The tide was coming in rapidly, so we transferred her body from the beach to the freezer unit off the kitchen, which is the best we could do. I've locked the unit, obviously, but at some point we'll need to inform the staff so that nobody wanders inside and gets a nasty shock."

"I'll take care of it," Mark said, in a voice subdued by sadness. "Poor girl. She had the rest of her life to lead."

"Yes, she did. Unfortunately, we now have an investigation to run, which is hardly ideal in the circumstances but there isn't much we can do about that. I'll need to interview every available guest and member of staff on site here, and I'll need a list of all the guests in attendance this evening, including those who've already gone home."

"I can put that together for you, as soon as the power's back up," Luke said.

"Good. If you could start lining up the staff, particularly those who worked closely with Danielle, I'll start with them. Before I do, I need to ask each of you whether you came across anything of interest during your searches?"

She turned first to Luke, who shook his head.

"Nothing of interest, just a couple of kids having fun in the shed," he said. "They hadn't seen Danielle, either."

She nodded, and turned to Gabi and Isolde. "Anything on your travels?"

"Nothing worth mentioning," Gabi replied.

"What about you, Mark? You searched Danielle's room, didn't you?"

He nodded, and thought of the photograph burning a hole in his pocket. Torn between family and other considerations, he placed the image on the table. "I found this," he replied, and Isolde felt a little jitter in the region of her chest as she looked at the image of a smiling Tristan with his arm around Danielle.

Sophie picked up the photograph and studied it more closely. "She had this in her bedroom?"

"Yes, tacked onto her wall, in the centre of a wider collage of magazine cut-outs featuring exotic destinations."

Unbeknownst to the others, during the course of searching Danielle's body, Sophie had found a note. It was barely legible, except for three words which read, "...there tonight—Tristan." She thought of this as she looked at the photograph, and then across at Isolde, and couldn't help but wonder what outcome the investigation would bring.

"Everybody will need to be questioned, including Tristan, so he will need to be found," she said. "One of you should do a quick recce of the main house, and check he isn't in his room. I need to get started with these interviews."

"I'll go with Isolde," Luke said, having seen her crestfallen face. "I'm sure he's probably just running late, but it doesn't hurt to check."

The bar manager, Simon Anstell, was a good-looking young man in his late twenties, with a rigid quiff to his hair and a set of white teeth which, despite the scarcity of light, could still be described as 'blinding'. Mark had set up a makeshift interview room in his own office, which resembled something from a bygone age now that it was lit by a number of candles borrowed from the spare candelabra in the ballroom.

Sophie set her phone to record, and hoped it would hold out for as long as possible.

"Mr Anstell, my name is Detective Inspector Sophie Keane, of the Devon and Cornwall Police," she said. "I'm sorry to tell you that one of your colleagues, Danielle Teague, was recently found dead on Haven beach. You have my sympathies."

Simon's face registered shock, but not quite as much as she would have expected to see. "I can't believe it," he said, robotically. "I mean, I know she's been missing for the past few hours, so, I suppose, I *can* believe it—"

She let him prattle, having learned that the best way to draw out a witness was by being silent. Usually, they felt compelled to fill the gap—often with all manner of interesting titbits.

"I'm asking routine questions, at this stage, Mr Anstell," she continued. "Rest assured, all of your usual civic rights and obligations still apply."

She rattled off the standard caution, and asked if he understood it.

"Yes, I understand. What do you want to know?" He began chewing the side of his thumb which, although a nasty habit, was not unusual, even for the most innocent persons. Being in the company of the police often made people nervous, usually for no good reason at all, and their little comfort tics weren't always a sign of guilt.

On the other hand, sometimes they were.

"If you could start by telling me how long you knew Miss Teague?"

"I don't know…five, six weeks?"

"And did you hire her yourself?"

"Actually, no. The order came from above."

"What do you mean by that, Mr Anstell?"

"Just what I say," he replied. "We got word the boss recommended her, so we hired her."

"When you say, 'the boss', do you mean Mark Williams?"

He shook his head. "No, Tristan."

Sophie's face remained impassive. "I see, and is that because they knew each other before Danielle started working here?"

"Must've done," he said. "To be honest, I don't know."

A certain defensiveness had crept into the man's voice, which Sophie found intriguing. "How did you find Danielle?"

He folded his arms, and leaned back in his chair. "What do you mean? She was a colleague, so, you know, I just thought of her that way."

"Ah-ha," Sophie said, and pursed her lips. "So, would you like to tell me when you and Danielle first got together?"

His face was a picture of guilt. “I’m married—”

“So?”

His lips clamped shut, and Sophie sighed.

“Look, Mr Anstell. I’ll let you in on a little secret: police officers see everything under the sun. I’ve seen the worst that humanity can create, so it’s highly unlikely that I’m going to be particularly moved by the shocking news that a young, attractive bar manager had an extra marital affair with his young, attractive employee. It happens every day, and I’m not here to judge. All I want to know is how she died, and the more I can find out about Danielle as a person, the easier that task will be.”

He let out a sigh, and nodded. “Okay, yeah. We had something casual going from the beginning.”

“Now we’re getting somewhere,” Sophie smiled. “So, perhaps you could tell me whether Danielle had any concerns, or anything else on her mind at all?”

He shrugged. “Same as everyone, really. She wanted a better life, more holidays, clothes…all that. She was a nice girl, you know, but you wouldn’t exactly say she was a conversationalist.”

Good enough to bed, not good enough to wed, eh? she thought, with distaste.

"How did she know Tristan Williams?"

"I dunno," he said. "I think her dad knew his dad, or something? Her family lives in Trebarwith, just down the road. Tristan's older than she was, by about ten years, but they kind of grew up together, played with the same circle of friends, that kind of thing."

Sophie nodded. "Do you know if there was ever anything romantic between them?"

"She never said as much," he replied. "But then, she'd hardly say that to *me*, would she?"

It was a fair point.

"Mind you," Simon added thoughtfully. "She'd started telling me she'd be off to London soon, because she'd found a sponsor who was going to take care of all of it for her. Well, that's likely to be him, isn't it?"

Sophie said nothing, but gave him an empty, professional smile.

"A few final questions, if I may, Mr Anstell. Could you tell me the last time you saw Danielle?"

"Yeah, sure. It was at the end of her shift, yesterday evening. She had worked the earlies, so she was off at seven."

"Is there anything else you think I should know?"

He shook his head. "Nah, can't think of anything. Can I go now?"

"Yes, but please remain available for further questions as and when they arise."

He stretched his arms, yawned, and then left. In the wake of his departure, Sophie was left with the strongest impression that she had, in fact, found an angel in Gabriel, if that one was any comparator.

CHAPTER 21

Luke and Isolde tried every obvious place to look for Tristan, including his mother's room. Meg was sleeping peacefully so the door was opened by her chaperone, Ellie, who told them that they hadn't received a visitor since they'd left the ballroom. She seemed genuinely concerned for Tristan's welfare, and that of his mother, and took the time to explain that her own mother had been widowed at an early age and had received all kinds of support from the Williams family over the years. That was why she was always happy to help out with any little tasks for Meg.

"It sounds to me like Tristan, his mother and his whole family are well-known and well-connected in the area," Luke said, once the door clicked shut again.

"Maybe he knows Danielle from the town or knows her family? Honestly, Isolde, it didn't seem to me to be a particularly romantic pose in that photograph."

She told herself to remain focused. "That may be the case, but she had that image on her wall, which goes to show it was meaningful to her in some way," Isolde replied. "I believe he had a meeting arranged with her, yesterday, although I have no idea what the meeting would have been about; I only know he was the person who alerted everyone to Danielle being missing—he was the first to think of it, and now he can't be found, either."

She felt sick at the thought.

"We should try to find the tunnel," she said. "He told me it was hidden behind a panel beneath the stairs."

"Which stairs? There are at least three staircases in the main building along, and more in the stable block," Luke pointed out. "Before we head off and try to be a couple of heroes, we should check in with Sophie and the others to let them know."

She acquiesced because it made good sense. "Luke, do you think Tristan's involved in Danielle's death?"

Her brother sighed. "I honestly don't know, Isolde. I know it looks suspicious that they were arranging meetings, and that she kept a picture on his wall, but there could be many reasons for that. It doesn't have to be sinister."

She nodded. "Every instinct tells me there's more to this than meets the eye. He's a good man; I feel it, in my gut."

"Is your gut reliable?"

"Usually."

"That's good enough for me."

Sophie looked up to see a young woman of around twenty-one hovering in the doorway.

"Come in and take a seat, please. What's your name?"

"Olivia Little," she replied.

"Thank you, Olivia. I'm DI Sophie Keane, and I'm investigating the death of one of your colleagues, Danielle Teague."

Olivia began to cry, and Sophie handed her a box of tissues.

"I'm sorry, it must have come as a dreadful shock."

Olivia nodded, and swiped her nose with the back of her hand. "I can't believe it," she said. "One day she's there and the next she's gone."

Sophie said nothing, because she was absolutely right; it was the nature of life and death, no matter how unpalatable. "Tell me about Danielle," she said. "How long have you known her?"

"We started here the same week," Olivia replied. "I have the room next to hers—room 8."

"I see," Sophie said. "Were you close?"

"Yeah, you could say that," Olivia replied. "I mean, it's only been a few weeks, but we really hit it off. She was a good laugh to be around, and she knew a thing or two about everything."

Sophie looked up from the notes she'd been scribbling. "What kind of thing—or two?"

"Oh, you know, Danielle always knew who was shagging who, or if anyone had nicked a bottle from the cellar...that kind of thing. She kept her ear to the ground, that one, and it paid off for her."

Sophie's ears sharpened. "What do you mean when you say it paid off for her, Olivia?"

"I mean she got some nice presents, didn't she? And that guy was gonna pay for her to go to London and get all set up. She told me he was gonna keep paying, he just didn't know it yet."

"Which guy was this, Olivia? Did she tell you a name?"

"No, but I heard him coming and going sometimes," she said. "It wasn't like when Sim—" She broke off, and went very red in the face.

"It's okay, I'm already aware of Simon and Danielle's relationship," Sophie said, and watched relief pass over her face. "You were going to tell me something else?"

Olivia nodded. "I was just going to say, the walls aren't very thick in that building, and I could hear when…you know, when Simon would visit." She turned an even deeper shade of red, from which Sophie surmised that the young woman was not quite so worldly as her late friend. "When this other guy came round, there was none of that, it was just a lot of hushed conversation," Olivia continued.

"Did you overhear what was said?"

She'd tried, Olivia thought.

"Only the occasional word," she replied. "I heard her say 'Tristan' a few times."

Sophie's heart sank. "In what context?"

"What do you mean?"

"I mean, how was he being discussed? Did you have the impression she was speaking *to* Tristan, there in the room, or speaking *about* him, while he wasn't there?"

"Oh," Olivia said, and pulled an expressive face. "I have no idea. It could have been either—but she had a picture of Tristan on the wall in her room. I think she quite liked him, but she never said they'd done anything."

Secrets, Sophie thought. *There were too many secrets here.*

"When did you last see Danielle alive?" she asked.

"Yesterday evening," Olivia replied. "I think she finished her shift at six, but mine was still going. I called out, 'see you later!' from behind the bar and she waved back, but she seemed in a hurry to be somewhere." Slow tears began to fall again. "All she really wanted was to go somewhere else, and be somebody else," Olivia whispered.

Sophie nodded, and thought that there was more to the case than accidental death or suicide; she was beginning to build a picture of a woman who'd been determined to go places, by fair means or foul, and thought she'd found something and somebody to help her. Perhaps her ambition had taken her too far…

"Sometimes, the ends don't justify the means," she murmured. "Is there anything else that you'd like to tell me, Olivia? Even the smallest thing could be important."

The young woman sniffed loudly, and shook her head. "No, I don't think…unless, I don't know if it's important or not, but you said even the smallest thing?"

"Yes, what is it?"

"Well, it's only that Danielle had learned a few things from some of the previous jobs she'd had at different hotels," she said. "One thing she always did was get a copy of the master key, and any other keys she thought would be useful. She had a locksmith friend who copied them within the hour and delivered them back to her."

"You're telling me she stole keys, had them copied and then returned them quickly before anyone noticed?"

Olivia nodded. "I don't want you to think she was a bad person," she said quickly. "She was just looking out for herself, and the keys came in handy a lot of the time."

Sophie could imagine.

Desk keys, door keys, safe keys…

"Do you know the name of her locksmith friend?"

Olivia shook her head. "No, she never said. Did I do the right thing telling you?"

"Yes, Olivia, you did. If I have any more questions, I'll get in touch."

Sophie watched the girl leave and sat for a moment in the dim candlelight, feeling like a heroine from a Dickensian novel. Tristan's name came up time and again in relation to Danielle Teague, but each time in circumstances that could easily be explained away. He no longer lived in the country, so there was little opportunity for them to have maintained any kind of friendship, even if their fathers had once been close. Danielle was dead, but there was no definitive cause other than suspected drowning; the wound on her head could have been sustained in the water, rather than on land, and without a forensics team Sophie couldn't make that kind of call herself. The interviews she'd conducted so far seemed to suggest Danielle had been worldly, and not averse to using people to get what she wanted. She also hadn't baulked at stealing keys and having them copied, but it didn't mean any of those factors had played any significant role in her death; she might simply have been caught out by the tide, after work. There was no smoking gun; no motive that she could tell, and, more to the point…

There was no Tristan.

CHAPTER 22

Luke and Isolde returned to the ballroom, where they found Sophie in discussion with their other friends. She broke off as they approached, and asked the question on everybody's lips.

"Any sign of Tristan?"

"None," Luke replied. "His mother hasn't seen him, either."

Sophie checked her watch again, and nodded. "That's a full hour behind the agreed schedule, so I think we're justified in progressing a wider search," she said. "Luke and Isolde have already checked the hotel rooms, but it's prudent to go over them again—Gabe? Would you mind doing that, please?"

"Gladly."

"When we all split up to search, Tristan offered to check the cave tunnel," Isolde reminded her.

"You mean Merlin's Cave?" Mark said.

"No, when he was showing me around Williams Cave, earlier, he told me there was an old smuggler's tunnel that runs beneath the house here. You can see the entrance to it from inside the cave, when the tide is low."

"I thought that was just a local legend," Mark replied. "Then again, I never lived or grew up here, this was always Meg and Harry's place. I suppose, when Tristan said he was checking the tunnel, I thought he meant the storm tunnel that runs between the house and the road. It was built to facilitate drainage, but sometimes people do go down there to smoke; it's big enough to stand in."

Isolde was adamant. "I don't think that's what he meant," she said. "He specifically told me that the tunnel starts behind some panelling in a cupboard beneath the stairs."

"Did he say which stairs?" Sophie asked.

"No, I'm afraid not."

"Then, let's look at each one in turn," she decided.

They decamped back out into the hallway, a group of six men and women bearing torches and a sense of urgency. They started with the main staircase off the reception hall, for it seemed the most obvious place, but there was no cleaning cupboard underneath.

"You're sure he said it was inside a cupboard beneath the stairs?" Luke said.

Isolde thought back, and then nodded. "Yes, that's what he said."

"It can't be this one, then," Sophie muttered, as she ran her hands over the panelling. "Let's try the next one. Mark? Which staircase would be most likely to have a cupboard underneath it?"

He held a hand to his head, and tried to think. "I—I don't know," he said. "What about the one in the housekeeping corridor?"

They started to move off, but then Gabi's voice stopped them. "Isolde and I went up those stairs not long ago, and I can't remember seeing any cupboard underneath," she said. "If you ask me, we should go in the opposite direction, towards the spiral stone staircase. It's one of the oldest parts of the house, and would have been contemporaneous to any tunnels that were built beneath the house."

Sophie nodded. "You're right. Which way is that?"

"Back through reception, on the southern corner of the house," Mark supplied. "I'll show you."

He led the way, and soon enough they came to the staircase, at the base of which was a small wooden door.

Sophie pulled it open.

Inside, there was a mop and bucket, a vacuum cleaner and various other cleaning materials for use by the housekeeping staff, but no obvious sign of a panelled entryway.

"Maybe it's another one," Luke said, dubiously.

"This is the one," Isolde said, and pushed forward to step inside the cupboard, where she proceeded to test all the walls for movement.

"How do you know?" Gabi asked.

"Because there's a draught," Isolde muttered, while she prodded and poked at all four sides. "You can feel it coming through the gaps in the panelling."

When her fingers touched the back wall directly beneath the stairs, she felt something shift.

"Here! It's moving!"

With a shove, the entire back panel of the cupboard came away to reveal a black hole of a tunnel, tall enough to walk in so long as a person bent over.

Isolde shone her torch inside and all around, but could see nothing but endless darkness.

"I'm going down," she said.

"Not on your own," Luke replied. "I'm coming with you."

"We all will," Mark said.

"One of us needs to stay here, in case of emergency," Sophie said.

"I'll do it," Gabi said, having never been a fan of confined spaces. "Be careful, all of you, and shout out if you need me."

One by one, they disappeared into the darkness.

Tristan knew that the water temperature in the cave was likely to be somewhere below twenty degrees Celsius, which meant that he would have about thirty minutes before his body would succumb to hypothermia. As soon as his body hit the waves, he moved his arms and legs vigorously, ignoring the cold shock that permeated his body and pushing the ticking clock from his mind as he made for the cave's entrance as quickly as he could.

He soon realised that the current inside the cave was like swimming in a whirlpool, where the force of the waves constantly churned the water, turning it around and around and making it an almost impossible task to break through for open sea.

After a few minutes, he knew he was making no progress, and would exhaust himself too soon if he tried to fight the current. Instead, he tried to gauge the natural movement of the water, wondering if he could allow the current to take him where he needed to go. It was an enormous risk—his body could have been thrown against the rocks at any time—but he could see no other alternative. He allowed himself to go limp and floated on the waves, which moved in a wide, sloshing circle from one side of the cave to the other. He tried to keep a picture of the cave in his mind while he estimated his position, and then, with another enormous leap of faith, chose his moment to strike out again, as the water came closest to the entrance and, beyond it, the beach where he and Isolde had raced one another across the sand.

He wanted to do that again.

He wanted to run and walk with her, to laugh and cry and share a life with her.

These thoughts came vividly to his mind, as did the knowledge that she'd probably put it down to the shock of hypothermia causing him to hallucinate.

Whatever the reason, he wanted the chance to find out.

CHAPTER 23

Isolde led the others down through the tunnel with single-minded precision. It was longer than anticipated, and had been built in a series of inclines down to cave level, each gradual incline measuring around a hundred feet in length before turning on itself to begin the next incline down, like a marble run. They counted four such inclines, until they heard the sea.

"Almost there!" she called out.

Soon enough, the iron gate came into view, but there was no sign of Tristan on either side of it. Beyond the gate, the rocky incline was now completely underwater as the sea level continued to rise, but their side occupied higher ground and so there was still time before they would need to beat a hasty retreat.

Isolde grasped the iron bars and tried to pull the gate open, but found it was locked by an old padlock on their side.

"Does anyone have a key for this?" she called back. "Mark?"

"I wouldn't know what it looks like, I'm afraid," he said, and dropped his torch to the rocky, compacted sand beyond the gate, where a set of footprints were still visible.

He moved his torch away so they would not be seen.

"It's obvious Tristan couldn't have come through here, if the padlock is locked from the inside," he said, reasonably. "I suggest we retreat and fan out to look for him. He's my nephew, so I'll take the cliffs, this time, and the beach or whatever's left of it."

"It's hard going out there," Sophie warned him. "It's better to go in pairs—"

"But it'll take longer to cover the ground, and he's been missing for almost an hour and a half," Mark said, in worried tones.

There was sense in that, so they agreed a solution.

"Isolde, someone needs to let Tristan's mother know that he's missing," Sophie said. "I'm sorry to ask it of you, but I think it might be better coming from you than from me if Mark is going to head straight out to search for him."

Isolde thought of Meg, and nodded.

"I'll let her know, then I'll come back and join the search."

They made their way back up to surface level, none of them having seen the pair of black trousers floating on the water.

After a steep walk uphill, they stepped back through the open panel and out of the cleaning cupboard, which Gabi had cleared out to make their passage easier.

"Oh, thank God," she said, as Luke re-emerged. "Did you find him?"

He shook his head. "There was no sign of Tristan," he said.

"What are we going to do?"

"Another search," Sophie replied. "It's the only thing we can do in the circumstances."

None of them would say it aloud, but each of them knew that, with conditions as they were, Tristan stood very little chance of survival if he found himself in open water or caught by the tide. Likewise, if he'd fallen somewhere on the pathways outside, he would succumb to exposure unless he was found before it was too late.

There wasn't a minute to lose.

"I'll head out now," Mark said.

"Be careful out there," Isolde replied.

He felt a moment's remorse, which was quickly squashed. "Thank you," he said gravely. "Let's hope we find him safe and well."

He made for the terrace doors one more time, telling himself there was one final task he needed to do. It was maddening, really, how it had come to this. First, that Danielle Teague would be so bold as to read his private papers and then have the *audacity* to demand payment in exchange for her silence, threatening to tell Tristan if he didn't comply.

He knew a better way to silence her, and it hadn't cost a penny.

As for his nephew...

He was exactly like Harry. Always poking his nose into places he shouldn't; asking questions, demanding answers, and never showing him the respect he deserved. If he'd only kept to his side of the business, and let him run his little venture in Cornwall, they'd have been a happy family.

What a pity.

Mark sighed, and began trudging across the lawns, yawning as he imagined the bed that awaited him once he'd made this final check. It was impossible to imagine that Tristan could have survived the cave—Danielle certainly hadn't—but he couldn't allow any loose ends and there would never be a better time than this for an accident to happen.

Tristan laboured through wind and rain against the sea, while his core temperature plummeted. All the while knowing that, if he couldn't reach a safe landing point soon, there would be no more tomorrows.

He was not prepared to allow that.

His muscles screamed and tore, his extremities numbed, and his lips began to turn blue, but still he fought his way towards the cliffs on Haven beach. The tide had dragged him far out of the cave, to begin with, and it had seemed history was repeating itself, for the current wanted to take him out to sea and away from those he loved. But, with some strength, determination, and a lot of luck, he found himself making headway against those forces dragging him back, and the rocks came into view again—nothing more than inky black shadows against the night sky.

Now, they were within striking distance.

He knew there was danger in being too close to them, but he had no choice; the sea dictated his journey, and he had to ride it as best he could. With an enormous surge of adrenaline, he made a bid for the nearest cluster, arms and legs pumping until a wave swept him up and against the stone. He clutched at whatever he could, refusing to be taken again, clinging on to scraps of seaweed and the hardened shells of limpets until he found the strength to drag himself up.

It took several attempts, and he cried out with the effort, but he managed to ease his way up, using the edge of his foot to climb the rock as he would have done on dry land—only, it was ten times harder when the surface was wet, and the sea continued to batter his body.

Shaking, shivering, he threw up the contents of his stomach there on the rocks, and then began to crawl, ordering his limbs to move and never to stop. He was on a cluster of bigger rocks that afforded some relative height above the sea, but to reach land he needed to cross a patch of low-lying rocks, hidden beneath the waterline. It made him sick again to think of having to go back in the water, but there was no choice.

He did what he needed to do and, as he summoned the courage, he thought of one thing.

Isolde.

CHAPTER 24

While the others went off in search of Tristan, Isolde made the long journey to his mother's room, where she had the unenviable duty to tell her that her son was missing. She'd had several offers of company, but had turned them down in favour of prioritising the search, which was more important. She therefore walked the long, dark corridors of the hotel alone, with only her torchlight for company.

And found that she wasn't afraid.

It was a revelation, of sorts; since the intruder had broken into her home, she'd lived in fear, jumping at shadows. It had taken all of her resilience to board the plane to Newquay, and she'd been exhausted by the effort. And yet, in the space of only a couple of days, she'd survived the sea and had pushed her body far beyond its own natural limits.

She'd also fallen in love.

It was remarkable how calm she felt about it, but then, extreme circumstances tended to normalise everyday things, so that they no longer seemed so overwhelming as they might once have done. It was a tragedy that, having come to the realisation, the object of her affection was not only missing but a person of interest in DI Keane's investigation.

She came to Meg's door, took a deep breath, and knocked.

Ellie answered, yawning hugely. "Hello?" she said.

"I need to speak to Meg," Isolde said.

"She's asleep—"

"No, I'm not," came a voice from within. "Is that Isolde? Come in!"

She stepped inside, to where a single glass hurricane lantern had been lit and put on the bedside table beside Meg, who was now sitting up in her bed, her legs covered with several layers of blankets for warmth.

"Come over here, and sit down," she said, patting the edge of her bed. "You look very cold…Ellie? Will you be a dear and fetch my big coat from the wardrobe over there, please?"

A moment later, Ellie produced a long woollen coat, which Meg pressed into Isolde's hands.

"I insist," she said. "Your hands feel like ice and your face is ashen, even in the candlelight."

"Thank you," Isolde replied, her voice thick with sudden tears. "I—I need to tell you something, Meg."

The older woman must have heard a note in her voice, for she clutched a hand to her throat.

"What is it?" she whispered. "Please, don't tell me it's—"

"Tristan is missing," Isolde said, her voice thick with tears.

There was a short, heavy silence following her announcement, and then Meg spoke so quietly Isolde strained to hear.

"I—I don't understand," she said. "How can he be missing? We were all together, in the ballroom, and he was fine. He said he'd come and see me, soon."

Isolde swallowed, and reached across the bed to take her hand. "One of the waitresses here, Danielle Teague, was missing first," she explained. "We split off to go in search of her, and, sadly, her body was discovered on the beach by Sophie and Gabriel, around an hour ago. When we first went off in search of her, Tristan offered to cover the tunnel and the unoccupied bedrooms here in the main house, but he never came back. I'm so sorry to have to tell you this, Meg, but you have a right to know. The others are out searching for him now, and I want to join them soon."

Meg could only shake her head back and forth as she tried to make sense of it all. "The tunnel?" she said. "I suppose he meant the old tunnel beneath the stairs, the one that leads to Williams Cave?"

Isolde nodded. "I think so, yes."

"Well, have you searched there?" Meg said, suddenly animated again. "If you have any trouble finding it, just ask Mark, because I'm sure he'll know—"

"He had no idea," Isolde said, wretchedly. "We found the tunnel anyway, and went inside to look for him. There was no trace, Meg."

Tristan's mother sank back against the cushions again, defeated.

"Where would he have gone?" she whispered. "It doesn't make any sense."

"It was the same with Danielle," Isolde said. "Nobody can understand how she managed to wash up dead on the beach, but she did."

It was the same, Isolde thought suddenly.

The same.

"There's some suggestion that Tristan was involved in Danielle's death," she added. "At least, it's looking as though he might have known how she came to die, or why." Meg opened her mouth to protest her son's innocence, but Isolde squeezed her hand. "I don't believe it, either," she said. "I think he might have known something, though; something Danielle told him or planned to tell him, perhaps? Maybe her death wasn't an accident after all, and Tristan somehow found out something about it?"

Meg listened, and a horrible thought struck her, deep in her core. "Why did Mark say he didn't know where the tunnel was?" she wondered aloud. "I'm sure he would have known; it wasn't a secret amongst the family."

They looked at one another with dawning recognition, and Isolde came to her feet.

"I hope we're wrong," she said.

"I hope so, too," Meg said, brokenly. "Be careful, Isolde."

Isolde left Meg's room at a run and hurtled back down the corridor to the main stairs, almost tripping down them in her haste to reach the ground floor. When she did, she burst into the reception area and found it empty, half-burnt candles the only evidence that somebody had once been there. She ducked into the ballroom and found none of their party, for they were in other parts of the house and grounds searching for Tristan, and the skeleton staff who remained were huddled together sleeping beneath a mountain of blankets.

She was on her own.

Isolde was still wearing Meg's woollen coat, so she hurried towards the terrace doors, which had been left with their key inside, this time, and let herself out into the storm. She ran into it, racing fearlessly through the wind and rain towards the cliffs, not thinking of the cliff edge nor of the danger that might await her at the other end.

She thought only of Tristan.

Tristan made it across the shallow rocks while his body wanted to fail, to give in and collapse, but he would not let it. He pushed himself to reach another cluster of larger rocks, which connected to the peninsula and would normally allow him to reach the beach and Merlin's Cave below. Unfortunately, the sand was completely immersed by the tide, and there was no safe access for him to cross towards the beach steps from his position.

He crouched there for a moment, scrubbing his hands over his skin, and decided there was only one clear route he could take, which was to scale the peninsula wall and try and pick up the steps that would lead him to the iron bridge at the top, and from there, to safety. On any other day, he might have been daunted by the prospect, but, after the lengths he'd already gone to, a little bit of rock climbing in the biting wind and rain, without any light or equipment, seemed like nothing at all.

It was good to keep a sense of humour about these things.

"Come on," he muttered to himself. "Keep moving."

He picked his way over the rocks towards the castle peninsula, and stared up at the sheer face of it. There would be no need to scale the full height, he thought, if he could manage to traverse around to the other side and pick up the steps, and the thought of it being less of a task was all the encouragement he needed.

Tristan planted his bare feet against the rock, took a firm hold, and began to climb.

CHAPTER 25

Mark Williams made his way down the wooden steps towards Haven beach, but could find no sign of his nephew in the water frothing against the cliffs. Nor had he seen him on the pathway from the hotel—Tristan wasn't there and, he very much hoped, wouldn't be for quite some time. It was always tricky, given the tidal currents, because a body could be washed many miles away or never seen again, while another one could come back to the shore by the end of the next day, as Danielle's had.

He wondered which it would be for Tristan.

It was difficult to pick out anything through the rainfall, but he'd brought his field glasses as a precaution and used them now to scan the sea and the rocks. He was about to turn back to the hotel, satisfied that Tristan was nowhere to be found, when he spotted a flash of movement on the underside of the castle peninsula.

He waited to see if the movement would come again.

It did.

"Unbelievable," he snarled, as he watched his nephew traverse the rocks, obviously heading for the steps on the other side.

He bared his teeth, and, thinking swiftly, turned to hurry back up to the top of the cliffs. From there, he could make his way to the castle and head Tristan off at the bridge, since that was the only possible exit he could take.

As Mark reached the entrance to the bridge, Isolde made it to the beach steps leading down to The Haven. She tried to see through the murky weather, looking for signs of life as he had done, but without the benefit of any field glasses or any knowledge that Tristan could be out there at all. She scanned the sea and the rocks below, but could see nothing, and her heart sank.

She was wrong.

But then, as she raised her eyes to look south towards the castle, there came a clap of thunder accompanying a bolt of lightning that broke through the clouds and lit up the sky, for seconds only, but just long enough for her to see a figure standing at the cliffside end of the bridge.

Mark.

The skies darkened again but she'd seen enough. She raced towards the bridge, not knowing what she would find, or how she could help; she only knew she had to try.

Tristan's arms were trembling badly as he made the final stretch from the rocks to the staircase that would take him up to the castle and across the iron bridge to the mainland. The tide prevented him from following the stairs directly across to the mainland from his position, but he told himself that he could manage a few more minutes…just a few more minutes. The climb had warmed his muscles sufficiently to raise his temperature, and he felt the slight change in his body, but once the climb was over, he would be at the mercy of the air temperature once again and would need to run back to the hotel to stay warm.

He thought this as he swung his leg across and onto the staircase, which he and Isolde had climbed only that morning. It seemed a lifetime ago, but he held the memory of it in his heart and mind as he struggled on, weak and injured, towards safety that was so close, now. When his legs threatened to fail him, he used his arms to drag himself up, and eventually reached the top. He stumbled past the mediaeval garden towards the entrance to the high bridge, no longer aware of the wind or the cold rain on his skin; aware of nothing but the need to survive and return home.

He let out a small cry of relief as he took his first step over the bridge, not caring that it rattled and whined as the gale rushed through its balustrades. He feared nothing, because he had survived everything. He took his first step, then another, the taste of freedom ripe on his lips.

When he had almost reached the centre of the bridge, Tristan thought he was hallucinating again. On the far side of the footbridge stood a man in a long, all-weather coat, hood turned up against the rain, his face in shadow. He appeared like a sentry on the other side, and it might have been the statue of Gallos come to life.

He shook his head, thinking that the injury and the exposure must have affected his mind, but, when he looked again, the figure was still there. In fact, it moved towards him now. He remained where he was, gripping the handrail, eyes trained on the stranger who approached him until he could see his face and know whether he was friend or foe.

In this case, he'd been both.

"Uncle? Thank God, it's you."

"We've been looking all over for you," Mark said, as he reached the centre of the bridge. "Let me help you."

He held out a hand to his nephew, who began to reach for it.

Then, his hand fell away again.

"How did you know I'd be here?"

Mark thought about telling him a useless lie, but, really, what was the point? He'd be gone very soon, and would have nobody to tell.

"I knew, because I put you here."

"*What*?" Tristan said. "*Why*?"

"Why?" Mark repeated. "Because you made it necessary, Tristan. You wouldn't leave well alone, would you? You forced my hand." He sighed, and rubbed a hand over his head. "Your mother will be devastated," he said, conversationally.

"It was all because of the money," Tristan realised, and felt sick again. "What happened, Mark? Did Danielle find out about your scheme?"

He nodded. "Resourceful young woman, I'll give her that," he said. "However, not quite resourceful enough, it seems. Unlike *you*, dear nephew. I have to tell you, part of me is proud to see you standing there, having battled it all to make it so very close to the finish line. Your father would be proud of you, as well—but then, he can tell you himself, when you meet him again very soon."

Tristan saw the intent clearly on the other man's face, and knew that his battle wasn't over.

Not yet.

Isolde ran towards the footbridge, flying as though the wind was beneath her wings and not a driving force against her.

When she came to the entrance, she saw both men immediately.

"*Tristan*," she whispered, and felt a surge of joy. "*Tristan!*"

She shouted his name to warn him, but the sound was lost on the night air.

By then, Mark had reached the centre point of the bridge, and the two men seemed to talk for a moment. Suddenly, the mood shifted, and they were grappling with one another, wrestling back and forth as one tried to overpower the other.

Isolde gripped the handrail for the second time that day, and experienced the same jitters in her stomach that told her to turn back. This time, she ignored them and stepped out onto the bridge, accepting the fear and pushing through it until she was not walking but running along the bridge towards them. She didn't pause to think but leapt onto Mark's back, arms banding around his neck like a vice, dragging him away from Tristan who was barely upright and almost beaten by fatigue.

Mark reared back, trying to shake her off, turning wildly and clawing at her skin until his nails dragged enormous welts along the length of her arms.

Still, she would not move.

She held on for as long as she could, feeling her hair being torn from her head, feeling his hard hands grab at her throat.

When she could hold on no longer, she released her grip and slithered onto the floor, where she narrowly avoided a large gap in the boards. By now, Tristan had recovered enough strength to stand again, and prepared himself for another attack.

But it did not come.

Instead, there was another clap of thunder, even louder than before, as the eye of the storm finally reached them. Mark turned his wrath upon Isolde, hard hands wrapping around her throat to lift her off her feet.

"Meddling...little...*bitch*!"

She struggled, clawing at his arms and his face, hitting out with her feet, but the hands around her throat were hard like iron and just as strong.

Tristan was in shock, his body wrecked from the sea and the struggle, but his mind drove him to his feet again with one last surge of adrenaline. He took a fistful of Mark's hair, pulled his head back and planted his fist in the man's face, again, then again, until his hands released Isolde and she fell to the floor gasping for air. He didn't stop then, understanding now it was a matter of self-defence and that, if he didn't win, the other man would.

Mark lunged at Tristan again, his eyes tinged with madness.

At the last moment, Tristan pivoted, using his back and his body to lift Mark from his feet. At the same time, a strong gust of wind rushed through the balustrades, and his whole body twisted on the wind.

Then, Mark Williams was falling, down and down to the rocks below, his fingers grasping for a lifeline but finding nothing but air.

CHAPTER 26

DI Sophie Keane made her way along to Meg Williams' room to check on the women in there, and to give Tristan's mother an update—which was to say, there was no update, at all. She never relished these moments in her career, but they were necessary.

She knocked at the door, and was greeted by a young woman in staff uniform.

"Ellie?"

"Yes, that's right. Are you looking for Mrs Williams?"

"And Isolde, if she's here?"

"Oh, no, she left about twenty minutes ago," Ellie replied. "She was heading down to the cliffs."

Sophie's senses returned to high alert, and she pushed past the girl to speak to Tristan's mother.

"Meg? Ellie has just told me Isolde went down to the cliffs," she said. "Why?"

Meg turned to look at the young woman with sad eyes. "Because she thinks Tristan's uncle is going to hurt him."

Sophie was shocked. "What? Why would she think that?"

"Because of the tunnel," Meg replied. "Mark's always known where it is. There was no reason for him to say otherwise."

Sophie filed that away for later. "When did she leave? Was she on her own?"

"She said she'd try to find help, but she'd go on her own, if she couldn't."

Sophie knew that the others had all gathered in the ballroom again, which meant only one thing.

Isolde was out there alone.

Tristan and Isolde watched Mark disappear into the ether, and both took an involuntary step forward to stop it, despite all the man had done. In the seconds that followed, Tristan fell to his knees, and she rushed forward to help him.

"Tristan! Oh, God. Please, stay with me," she said, and shouldered out of his mother's heavy coat to wrap it around him instead.

Her fingers brushed his skin, and found it icy cold.

"Come on," she said. "You need to get up and walk, Tristan! Do you hear me? *Walk*!"

He was barely responsive, but she found strength for the both of them. Isolde took one of his arms and wrapped it around her neck, put another arm around his waist, and then heaved him up, feeling her slim body protest beneath the muscled weight of him.

"Now, Tristan! I need you to stand, *now*!"

He must have heard her, for he pushed himself up to a half-standing position.

"Good enough," she puffed, and half carried him, half dragged him back across the footbridge.

Once they were on the other side, he collapsed again, and she knew then that they would never make it back to the hotel.

Not without help.

No sooner had Isolde thought it than help arrived.

She saw them running along the headland, her brother and his friends, shouting and waving to her. She couldn't hear their voices, but she saw their arms and knew what they must be saying.

We're coming!

She held Tristan tightly against her, his body still convulsing with small shudders as she rubbed the skin beneath the woollen coat, to create warmth.

"Hold on," she whispered to him.

When they arrived, she barely held back tears. "He's freezing," she said. "We need to get him back as quickly as possible."

Luke said nothing, but simply stepped forward and, with a strength he didn't know he had, slung Tristan over his shoulder.

"I'll see how far I can go," he said, and set off at a steady pace up the pathway.

"I can take a turn whenever you need it," Gabriel said, and kept pace with Luke to make sure he didn't trip on the pathway.

Sophie, Gabi and Isolde followed in the rear, watching their joint effort.

"A few good men," Sophie murmured.

Isolde nodded, unable to speak.

"Where's Mark?" Sophie asked.

"He fell from the bridge," Isolde replied, and shuddered at the memory. "They were fighting when I got there, and Mark was overpowering Tristan. I tried to intervene, but he threw me off and started attacking me. Tristan fought him off, and, the next thing we knew, he'd gone over the side of the bridge."

"He wasn't pushed?"

"No, it happened as Tristan was defending himself and me."

There were still questions unanswered, Sophie thought, but they could wait until morning—so long as Tristan was alive, by then.

As soon as they set Tristan down on one of the leather sofas in the library, Isolde began issuing orders.

"Luke? There's a fire laid out in the grate there, if you could please light it," she said. "There are matches in the cleaning cupboard, I saw them when we were in there."

He nodded, and dashed off in search of them.

"Gabi? We need more blankets to keep him warm," she said.

Her sister-in-law hurried away to find them.

"Can anybody find out if there's a doctor in the hotel?"

She laid a hand over his neck, and then stood up to begin undressing, while the others looked on in surprise.

"It helps with heat transference," she said, and crawled beneath the blankets to wrap herself around his cold body without any self-consciousness whatsoever.

Gabi came back with a stack of blankets and began piling them on.

"What else can we do?" Luke asked.

"Sugary food," she demanded. "He needs something sugary to eat, if he can."

Gabriel hurried back to the ballroom, where there had been chocolates aplenty, and returned bearing a plateful.

Isolde crushed one of them until it was mush, and then rubbed it against Tristan's lips.

He tasted it, so she gave him some more.

"I did a news segment once, all about how to deal with suspected hypothermia," she explained. "I hope I'm remembering the right things."

By then, Luke had lit the fire, and it began to crackle.

They stayed like that awhile, Isolde holding Tristan in her arms as he continued to breathe, letting him take her body heat while the fire worked on his extremities and the blankets insulated whatever heat they could generate.

Sophie returned after completing a door-to-door enquiry, with the bad news that there was no medical doctor in the hotel. The power remained down, the lines were dead and there was no signal to the outside world.

"How far does the tree block the road?" Isolde asked.

"It's the whole way," Luke said, with regret. "You can't get past it."

"You could," she said. "In your Land Rover. It can practically climb stairs."

Luke thought of the grounds, and of any potential exit routes, then shook his head.

"I'm sorry, Isolde. You know I would take him, if I could, but there's no way to get a vehicle out besides the main entrance. There's a stone wall around the full perimeter of the grounds, and there isn't another entrance because the house faces the sea."

Isolde knew it, but it didn't relieve her devastation.

Then, Tristan spoke.

It was only a single word, but they all heard it.

He said, '*Isolde*'.

"I'm here," she murmured. "You're safe."

She kept him talking for a while, mumbled conversation that made little sense, but kept his mind active when it might have wanted to shut down. Slowly, his body warmed, and he fell into an exhausted sleep. Only then did they move him to his own room, where Isolde lay beside him throughout the night.

CHAPTER 27

Sunday morning

Tristan opened his eyes to find his room bathed in the misty pink and purple hues of dawn. Everything hurt, from his head to his feet, but his first thought was to thank whichever power above that he was alive and well enough to feel it.

His second thought was that he was not alone.

He turned to find Isolde lying in the bed beside him, her hand holding his, even in sleep. He watched her for a long moment, his eyes running over her face in the early morning light, committing it to memory like a starving man.

As if she'd felt it, her eyes opened.

"Tristan," she whispered.

Isolde leaned forward to press the gentlest of kisses to his lips.

"I thought…you were so ill, I thought you might not come through—"

She began to cry then, unable to stem the flow of tears any longer.

"Shh," he said, through cracked lips. "Don't cry. Don't cry, Isolde."

"How are you feeling?" she asked.

He pulled a face. "Everything hurts. I think my wrist is sprained, and there's a cut on the back of my head where my uncle bludgeoned me."

"It was definitely him, then?"

"He admitted it," Tristan replied. "Last night, on the bridge, he more or less told me he'd killed Danielle, and that he tried to use the same method with me." He paused, as the memory of it replayed in his mind. "He must have attacked me from behind, and then dragged me to the cave side of the tunnel gate," he said. "Then, he locked the gate so I couldn't get back through the tunnel. That left only two options for me: to swim and risk drowning, or to stay put and risk drowning.

I didn't like the sound of either of them, but I went for Option A."

"He must have done the same thing to Danielle," Isolde said. "She didn't stand a chance."

"I think she might have been blackmailing him," Tristan said, and then, noticing the marks on Isolde's arms and neck, pushed himself up so that he could get a better look at her.

"You're badly hurt," he said. "Have you had those cuts seen to?"

She tugged her top down her arms, so her torn skin would no longer be visible.

"Gabi used some antiseptic and I've taken painkillers," she said. "They'll heal."

The events of the previous evening came back to him in fits and bursts, and he experienced a flash memory of Isolde launching herself onto his uncle so that he would have a chance of survival. Her bravery had saved him, a second time.

"I'm here because of you," he said.

"No, you're not. You did all the hard work—"

"Because of you," he repeated. "I wanted to survive because I had a reason to. My family and friends, yes—but mostly you, Isolde."

She brushed his hair back from his forehead.

"Did you ever see the movie *Speed*?" she asked him.

Tristan laughed at the change of direction. "Ah, I think so? Is that the one where they're stuck on a bus with a bomb on it?"

"That's the one."

"Why do you ask?"

"Well, at the end of it all, Sandra Bullock's character says to Keanu that relationships borne out of high-octane events never last."

"That's interesting, but what does it have to do with us?"

"Isn't it the same?"

He shook his head. "You began conquering your fears from the moment you touched down in Newquay," he said. "You couldn't cross the bridge yesterday morning, but by the evening you were running across it to help me, in the darkness and in a storm. While I'm grateful that you did it, that isn't the reason I've fallen in love with you. I fell for your character, which is strong in adversity. You never let yourself be beaten. You're resilient, kind and loyal, aside from all your other attributes.

You care about your family, and you cared for mine, when I couldn't. You're a lovely woman, Isolde Malone, and I want to be with you."

Tears came to her eyes again, but they were not unhappy.

"I'll never forget our swim the other day, or the sight of you fighting for me on the bridge," he continued. "Just as I won't forget the beautiful, hazy memory of you holding me in your arms last night to warm me and keep my core temperature where it needed to be. They're all high-octane memories, Isolde, but they aren't the reasons I love you. I could list them, but I think it comes down to the simple fact that we're right for one another. I can't explain it."

As she listened to him, Isolde remembered the fear she'd felt when she thought he was dead, or when she thought she'd been too late to help him. She'd thought of all the time they'd never share, all the memories they'd never make, and, in remembering, she realised that the perilous circumstances they'd been in were only trappings. Tristan could have been a man she'd met over dinner somewhere, without any other hardships or obstacles to overcome, just like many of the nice men who'd taken her out over the years, but, if she never gave them, or him, or love, a chance, then she'd forever be stuck on that metaphorical bridge and unable to cross.

She took a deep breath, and said the words that felt true.

"I love you, too."

He smiled, and drew her in for a kiss. "There," he whispered against her lips. "That wasn't so hard, was it?"

"What do we do now?"

"I think it's generally acceptable to live 'happily ever after'," he replied. "But, until then—"

He broke off.

"What is it?" she said urgently.

"I had no idea you were half naked in bed beside me, this whole time," he said, with a gleam in his eye. "I feel that I've let down the whole of mankind by not taking advantage."

She laughed. "I can see you're feeling better," she said, giving him a playful swat on the arm. "If you get well soon, maybe I'll let you take advantage. How does that sound?"

He raised a hand to touch her face.

"I warn you, I'm about to make a miraculous recovery."

The morning sunlight had washed away the horrors of the night before, leaving blue skies overhead. From the bedroom window, Tristan and Isolde could hear the fallen tree being cut into parts to allow access for the National Grid and other services to enter, including a doctor for Tristan so that he could be properly checked over, and the Coroner's Office, who needed to come and collect the body of Danielle Teague. Were it not for the continued lack of power, the residents of the Tintagel Hotel might have thought it had all been a dream—or, in the case of some, a nightmare.

One person who held no illusions was DI Keane, whose investigation was far from complete. The facts as she knew them were that two people were dead, both in suspicious circumstances and one without any witnesses—and the only person common to both was Tristan Williams. As soon as she heard he was awake and lucid, she made her way to his room to seek the answers she needed.

Isolde answered the door. "Morning! Have you come to see the invalid?"

Sophie smiled, but it didn't quite reach her eyes. "Yes. May I come in?"

"Of course," Isolde said, not quite understanding the formality. "Tristan's awake now."

"Hello, Sophie," he said, and raised a hand in greeting. "Thank you for your help, last night."

She pulled a chair up to the side of his bed, and seated herself. "That's why I'm here," she said. "There are still quite a few unanswered questions, which I'm hoping you can help me with—if you're well enough, that is?"

Tristan frowned, but nodded. "I think so, yes."

"I should tell you that you're entitled to have a lawyer present, so we can postpone this until another time if that's what you would prefer?"

"What's all this about, Sophie?" Isolde cut in. "You saw for yourself what happened last night—"

"No, I didn't," came the reply. "None of us saw what happened aside from you two, and Tristan's late uncle. As for Danielle, we don't know how she died. Drowning seems most likely, but how that came to happen is anybody's guess. I have to investigate all avenues fully, which I hope you understand."

"I'm happy to tell you whatever I can remember," Tristan said. "I have nothing to hide."

"Would you like me to leave?" Isolde asked.

He shook his head. "As I said, I have nothing to hide."

Sophie took out the notebook she'd used the previous evening. "Firstly, could you begin by telling me how you knew Danielle Teague?"

"I'd say I barely knew her at all," he replied. "Danielle is the daughter of one of my father's old friends, whom I keep in touch with because he's a chess player and so am I."

It was news to Isolde, and she wondered what else they would come to learn about one another.

"Danielle was more than ten years younger than me, so we didn't spend time growing up together, aside from the occasional neighbourly barbeque or dinner, that sort of thing."

"Go on," she murmured.

"She contacted me out of the blue—around three months ago, I think," he said. "She was looking for summer work, so I forwarded her name to Mark and asked him to find something for her, as a kindness to an old friend."

"Was that the extent of your relationship?"

"*Yes*, it was," he snapped, and then immediately regretted the pain in his head. "Why do you ask?"

"When a search was made of Danielle's room, we found this," Sophie said, and retrieved the photograph that had been tacked to her wall.

Tristan looked at it through a fog of painkillers.

"I don't even remember when this was taken... from the look of me, and of Danielle, this must have been a few years ago. Possibly five or six?"

Then, it came to him.

"I remember now—this was taken at her father's sixtieth birthday party, which they held in their back garden in Trebarwith. You can see the bunting in the background."

Sophie looked again, and saw that he was right. She could check the details when she spoke to Danielle's family, but so far his story rang true.

"When was the last time you spoke with Danielle, or saw her alive?" she asked him.

"It would have been at around five o'clock on Friday evening, just after we had cocktails in the library. She called me over and asked if I had some time at the end of her shift, because she needed to talk to me about something important. I asked her what it was, but she said she'd rather speak in private. I agreed to meet in her room at six-thirty."

"And did you?"

"I was running late, because I was enjoying dinner with Isolde," he said, with a smile for the woman beside him. "I remembered the time and hurried over to knock on her door, but there was no answer. I assumed she hadn't bothered to wait, or had been held up herself, so I planned to speak to her the following day instead. When I asked around for her the next morning, I was told she hadn't turned up for her shift."

"You already told me last night that you went back to her room in the afternoon to look for her again, and this time let yourself in using a master key to check," Sophie said. "Why did you feel compelled to do that?"

"I was worried," he said. "She seemed to be missing, as I told you."

"Yes, but, as your uncle said, plenty of seasonal staff go astray, and a man in your position surely doesn't concern himself with individual staff members?"

"I do if they're the daughter of a family friend, and if she'd seemed upset the last time I saw her," he replied. "She wanted to tell me something, but never had the chance."

"And do you know or suspect what that something was?"

"Yes," he replied. "I suspect it has to do with my uncle's embezzlement of funds from the business, which I've suspected for some time."

"Did your uncle know that you were aware?"

"No," he replied. "Given his approach to problem solving, if he'd been aware that I was looking into his management, I would probably be dead. He tried twice, and that was only as a preventative measure, to stop me digging into his affairs."

Sophie raised an eyebrow. "To be clear, you're alleging that your late uncle, Mark Williams, attempted to kill you?"

"I'm not alleging, I'm stating a fact. First, I believe he tried to kill me by dropping a stone on my head. When that didn't work, he tried again, by attacking me from behind and then leaving me for dead in a tidal cave. He admitted the last part while we were on the bridge, when he would also have thrown me over the side if he could. He might have done, if Isolde hadn't intervened. As it was, he attacked Isolde, as you can plainly see from the bruises on her arms and throat, and I pulled him off. We fought, and he went over the side."

"Without any witnesses or material evidence, I have only your word for this version of events?"

"Why would I lie?"

Sophie didn't answer, but took out another small plastic bag, this time containing the scrap of a note she'd found on Danielle's body. "Can you read what this says?"

Tristan could just make out his own name, in permanent marker, and the tail end of a message that appeared to be arranging a meeting.

"Where did you find this?"

"On Danielle's body, after she was recovered from the beach," Sophie replied.

Tristan shook his head. "I didn't write any notes to Danielle," he said, firmly. "I don't write notes, as a rule. We live in the digital age, for God's sake."

"That may be, but you can see that, from my perspective, this looks like evidence of a note sent to Danielle telling her to meet you at a certain time and place—possibly the place she died."

He ran an agitated hand through his hair. "I had absolutely no reason to want her dead," he said. "Can you think of a single one?"

"There are many reasons why a man might be interested in a young woman like Danielle Teague," Sophie replied. "Sex, being the most obvious one. Accidents can happen."

He glanced at Isolde, then back at Sophie. "Look, I had no interest in Danielle in that way," he replied. "If there was a note, then somebody else put it there, not me." He knew who it was, too. "It must have been my uncle," he said. "Maybe he was hoping to pin her death on me?"

Sophie took the note back, and returned it to her pocket. "We can hardly ask him, can we? On the topic of your uncle...disagreements can easily get out of hand. Who's to say the fight on the bridge wasn't instigated by you, rather than him?"

"I saw them, with my own eyes," Isolde put in, angrily. "It was obvious—"

"Could you hear their conversation when you arrived on the scene?" Sophie interjected. "Did you see their body language or facial expressions from your position at the far end of the bridge?"

"Well, no—"

"And that's exactly what any good prosecutor would say," Sophie told them. "Listen to me, and understand why I'm asking you these uncomfortable questions. It's to clear the innocent from all suspicion. Imagine if I did a half job of this, and the locals started to talk. Danielle's family would hear about this photograph, about the man who planned to take her to London, about the job offer and about the meetings you'd arranged to have with her, and start wondering. That's all it takes, in the beginning, for a seed to grow. It only takes a community to be without definitive answers, and they'll start looking for them, sometimes in the wrong places."

Isolde understood then, and respected Sophie all the more for the job she did.

"I understand," she said. "I'm sorry I lost my temper."

"There's no need to apologise," came the reply. "But you can see my predicament here. We need something that would prove your allegations beyond all doubt, not only for my benefit but for yours."

"How can I do that?" Tristan asked her, in frustration. "I didn't happen to have any recording equipment on me, at the time."

Sophie thought for a moment. "I'll be digging into your uncle's finances, as soon as I get back to civilisation, where there's hot coffee and an internet connection," she said. "I'll be looking into Danielle's, too, which should throw up some information about who, if anyone, had been paying her."

"What about the key?" Isolde said, suddenly.

"What key?" Tristan asked.

"The key to the padlock on the iron gate, down in the tunnel," she said. "If Mark's the one who bludgeoned you down there, he'd have been the one to lock the padlock behind you, as well. If you find the key, surely the police forensics team can check it for prints?"

Sophie was impressed.

"If we were lucky, and could lift some clear prints, that would be fairly definitive, I'd say. Especially since your uncle disclaimed any knowledge of the tunnel before last night. It would be hard to explain how his prints came to be on the key, otherwise, wouldn't it?"

"There's just one problem with that," Tristan said.

They looked at him.

"I've no idea where that key would be. In a house this size, it could be anywhere."

Sophie smiled for the first time. "Leave it to me—I'm going to walk into the village and put a call through to my team. They'll turn the place over to find it."

"We can help?" Isolde offered, but Sophie shook her head.

"This house is a crime scene, now," she reminded them both. "It was different last night, when we were cut off by the storm and there was an urgent search needed for missing persons." She came to her feet. "The best thing you can do is get well, and leave the investigating to the professionals."

Once the door shut behind her, Tristan blew out a long breath and turned to Isolde. "I want you to know, I didn't hurt Danielle."

"I know," she murmured. "So does she."

CHAPTER 28

Once the fallen tree was pulled aside with the help of a local farmer and his tractor, the cavalry arrived in force. Leading the charge was one Police Constable Alex Turner, Sophie's right-hand man, general dogsbody, and good friend. He was tall and lanky, with a boyish face that gave the impression of being a man much younger than his years, and was possessed of the kind of insubordinate nature she'd nurtured from their first meeting and could only be proud of.

Turner unfolded himself from a squad car, looked around at the old pile, and made a low, whistling sound. "Nice stack of bricks," he said. "Is the power back on?"

"Not yet, but they're making good progress," she replied.

"You look like you've been dragged through a hedge backwards."

That was all the deference Sophie had come to expect. "I've been manhandling bodies, scouring cliffs and scampering through tunnels, all without so much as a cup of tea or a hobnob," she said. "What's your excuse?"

"Rough night, last night," he said, and stifled a yawn. "I went out with that surf instructor guy I've been seeing, but we ended up doing a round of shots—" He gave a delicate shudder at the memory. "It was fun at the time, but it feels like I've got a marching band going around my head now."

"Ah, the folly of youth," she drawled. "I suppose you're ready to see the body now, then?"

He turned green at the gills. "Have pity," he said. "Besides, I thought there were two bodies?"

She nodded, and waited until one of the hotel staff had passed by before continuing. "We found what was left of Mark Williams washed up on the rocks at the base of the castle peninsula first thing this morning," she said quietly. "The other body belongs to Danielle Teague, aged twenty-four, formerly a staff member here at the hotel. We found her late last night on Haven beach, but she'd been dead at least twenty-four hours by then."

"You said you needed forensics to come urgently," he said. "They're on their way, and making noises about it being the weekend."

"Bodies can turn up any day of the week," she muttered. "They don't get a copy of the roster for Scenes of Crimes."

Turner grinned. "Tell that to Irwin," he said, referring to their senior Scenes of Crimes examiner. "How do you want to approach this?"

Sophie thought of the people within the house, and of the competing demands of her role. "I want you and another constable to interview all the remaining guests," she said. "I made a good start with the staff, and those closest to Danielle, last night. I'll show you my notes with their statements. After then, we need to find a key."

"A key?"

"Yes, Turner, a key. I'll explain everything, but first, I have something more pressing to attend to."

"What's that?"

"My stomach," she said, and let it guide the way.

As it happened, Sophie was not the only person to be feeling hunger pangs. When she and Turner made their way through the reception area, their noses were assailed by the potent smell of charred meat, and immediately their mouths began to water.

"I wish I could be a vegetarian," he remarked, with genuine regret. "But why does chicken have to taste so good?"

"I ask myself the same thing, every day," Sophie replied, and sniffed the air.

They followed the scent outside, where Luke had procured a barbeque, fired it up with coals and was now searing meat and vegetables of varied description for a waiting crowd of hotel residents. Beside him, a small crowd of men including Gabriel had gathered to watch the meat cook, and Sophie could almost hear the David Attenborough commentary running through her head.

And here, we have the classic hunter-gatherers, circling the kill...

"What is it about barbeques, Turner?" she asked.

But he'd already wandered off to join the rest of them.

She scanned the crowd who'd gathered on the terrace, and it called to mind wartime scenes, from people waiting in line for a sausage sandwich to those gathered around the ornamental fire pit, where a large pot was boiling water for tea and coffee. There was a sense of community, despite all the darkness of the night before, and it warmed her heart to see it.

"Would you like a cup of tea?" Gabi approached her with two steaming mugs.

"I won't say no," Sophie replied, with a smile. "The power should be back on, shortly."

Gabi nodded, and sipped her tea. Sophie did the same, and then pulled a face.

"What kind of tea do you call this?"

"Oh, sorry, it's a herbal blend. Isolde brought it over from Ireland and I've got a bit of a taste for it, now."

Sophie wrinkled her nose, but decided a hot drink was still a hot drink, so she'd force it down for the sake of politeness.

"How's Tristan doing? I went to see him earlier, but he was sleeping."

"He's recovering well," Sophie replied. "He's very lucky to be alive."

Gabi nodded, and smiled at the sight of the four men arguing over whether the sausages were cooked through. "I heard what happened to Mark," she said. "I was going to say it's a tragedy, but it's hardly that, if he was planning to do the same thing to his nephew."

Sophie didn't comment on that, but continued to sip her tea. "We found his body, this morning," she said. "The coastguard helped to transfer it to the mortuary, and the coroner is due any minute to collect Danielle."

Both women looked up at the blue skies speckled with fluffy white clouds, then back across the lawn to where a small puff of smoke indicated that a sausage had been burnt.

"I can hardly believe last night happened," Gabi said. "The ground is wet, and there are bits of fallen trees and rubbish strewn across the lawns, but when I woke up this morning it felt unreal."

Sophie had heard that many times before, from those with secondary trauma. "It was a hard night," she said. "Learning of Danielle's death was traumatic enough, especially having searched for her. Then, Tristan's disappearance was another worry, as was the question of whether he would recover from the exposure to cold. These are no small things. It's normal to feel a sense of unreality."

Gabi nodded, and polished off her tea. "Another one?" she asked.

"Thanks, but I'll switch to coffee. I have to pay a visit to a grieving family, and herbal tea isn't going to cut it."

CHAPTER 29

Isolde looked across at Tristan, who was sleeping peacefully in his bed, and thought that he looked younger, somehow. The muscles of his face were relaxed thanks to a mild sedative supplied by the local doctor, who had checked his vitals, tended his wounds, and pronounced him well enough to stay at the hotel under supervision, with the proviso that he attend hospital later that afternoon for a thorough check. It helped that Tristan was awake and lucid, and had been for hours, which was a strong indication that he had avoided hypothermia or concussion. Meg had returned to her own room to rest, having sat with her son throughout the morning, but Isolde remained to watch over him.

Presently, there came a loud beeping noise, and the lights came back on, eliciting a distant cheer from somewhere downstairs. Tristan slept on, so Isolde moved around the room turning off the lights and regulating the heat, and then reached for her phone, which seemed to have regained its network connection since the previous evening's blackout.

It rang, immediately.

She swallowed the small jolt of surprise, and, seeing that it was Owen, her producer, she answered the call and kept her voice low. "Owen?"

"Isolde! I've been trying to call you all morning," he said. "How's things?"

A hysterical laugh bubbled up, which she barely contained. "Have you got a minute?" she asked him.

"Several, in fact."

"Well, settle in, because you're not going to believe this."

He listened as she told him about the previous night's events, and, when she was done, he let out a gusty sigh. "It sounds to me like you should come back to work—for a rest."

She laughed, assuming he was joking.

"I'm not kidding, Isolde," he said, with a note in his voice. "You've only been gone a couple of days, but already the ratings are way down. Maeve has done her best, but she's not really cutting it as a substitute."

Isolde was surprised. "I didn't know that Maeve was standing in for me," she said, with a small frown. "I haven't heard from her…then again, there's been a power cut, so that's not her fault."

"I'm sure she's tried," Owen said. "But the fact is, we need you back, Isolde, if you're well enough?"

Isolde realised that, aside from a bit of a headache the previous day, which could have been due to tiredness or the after-effects of her cocktail consumption, she hadn't suffered a single migraine since she'd been in Cornwall—nor had she suffered any blurred vision or general aches and pains.

"I'm well enough," she said, but then her eye fell on Tristan's sleeping form. She watched his chest rise and fall, and remembered their words to one another not long ago.

What would it mean, if she returned to Dublin?

She had a life there, a career, a home. She couldn't just give them all up.

He had a life in New York, a career and a home, too.

What were they going to do?

Doubts began to creep in again, and she told herself that his declaration of love was most likely influenced by feelings of gratitude. How could either of them be sure of their feelings for one another in the aftermath of such extreme circumstances?

Perhaps a bit of distance wouldn't hurt.

"I can be back tomorrow," she said. "In time for the evening show, if you like."

"You're a lifesaver," Owen gushed.

"That's what I hear."

Sophie set her constables to work scouring the hotel for an iron key, with strict instructions not to leave any stone unturned and, when they found it, to hold it with extreme care using nitrile gloves at all times so as to preserve any fingerprints. In the meantime, she and Turner made the short journey to Trebarwith to see Danielle Teague's family and deliver the worst news of their lives, which could not be put off any longer.

They lived in a cosy, white-painted cottage in the centre of the village, which had been built in the typical style of that part of the county, being short, squat and hardy enough to withstand the changing weather. As they approached the front door, they heard a radio playing eighties hits somewhere within, alongside the sound of a vacuum cleaner.

Sophie drew in a fortifying breath, glanced at Turner, and then raised her fist to knock.

A second or two later, the vacuum cleaner was turned off, and the door swung open to reveal a woman in her fifties dressed in workout gear. She wore a friendly smile on her face, which began to slip like a waxwork model as they introduced themselves.

"Mrs Teague?"

"Yes," she replied, eyes darting between them. "Who're you?"

But she knew. Her heart knew, long before her mind did.

"I'm Detective Inspector Sophie Keane and this is Police Constable Alex Turner. We're from the Devon and Cornwall Police. May we come in, please?"

They took out their warrant cards, which she barely looked at.

"What is it?" she whispered. "What's happened?"

Sophie glanced around the street, where people were slowing down to rubberneck.

"If we could speak more privately, Mrs Teague?"

The woman nodded, and stumbled back into the house. They followed, and shut the door behind them. In the background, Whitney Houston had begun to sing about knowing when a man truly loved her but, for once, nobody felt like dancing.

"Who is it, love?"

The music stopped, and Adam Teague wandered into the living room, which was directly off the front door.

"Oh, hello," he said, cheerfully. "Can we help you?"

"Mr Teague?"

"Yes, that's right. Are you selling something?"

"No," Sophie replied, and introduced them both again. "We're here about your daughter, Danielle."

"What's she gone and done, this time?" he asked, with the air of a long-suffering father. "Look, my Dani's not bad, she's just misguided. Never knows when to stop, that's all it is. Now, if you'll just let me have a word with her, you have my word—"

Sophie couldn't let him rumble on any longer. "Mr and Mrs Teague, we regret to inform you that your daughter, Danielle, was found dead on Haven beach during the storm last night. You have our deepest sympathies."

They looked at her as though she'd grown two heads.

"*What*?" Irene Teague said. "I don't—I'm sorry, I don't understand—"

"There must be some mistake," Adam said. "Our Dani is working up at the Tintagel Hotel."

But Tristan had called them, on Friday, looking for her.

He thought of that phone call, and his stomach began to twist.

"Look," he said, a bit desperately. "I know Dani was missing on Friday, but she can be a bit flighty at times. She might've hopped off work, or met some boy...that's probably what's happened."

"I'm sorry, Mr Teague, but there's no mistake. Your daughter was identified, and some of her personal effects were found with her. We're very sorry."

Something about the finality of her words, the kind but unyielding way in which they were imparted, must have penetrated. Their faces crumpled, and Adam moved across to put an arm around his wife's shoulder and lead her to the sofa, before she fell down.

"*Danielle*?" she whispered. "My girl. My girl."

"What happened?" Adam asked them, in a voice choked with tears. "How—how did it happen?"

Sophie swallowed, and fixed her eyes on the sofa. "We believe she was drowned, however her death is currently classified as 'suspicious' because we have reason to believe she might have been murdered."

"Who'd want to kill her?"

"We're investigating the answer to that question, Mr Teague. We were hoping you might be able to tell us something of her life, the people she spent time with…and how you know the Williams family."

"The Williams family? Well, of course, Harry was a friend, God rest him. I knew his wife, Meg, and I keep in touch with his son, Tristan, who's turned out to be just like his father. He plays chess, so he comes around and has a game occasionally."

"Did he and Danielle spend time together?"

"Not really," Adam replied. "They knew one another, but they moved in different circles and had different interests. Besides which, Tristan's always away, working. We only see him if he happens to be back in the area visiting his mum, or one of the hotels."

Which was exactly what Tristan had told her, Sophie thought.

"Why d' you want to know about Tristan?" Irene wondered. "He isn't involved, is he?"

"Just being thorough, Mrs Teague. We have to ask a lot of questions to build up a picture of what happened."

Silent tears began to roll down Irene's face, and Turner rose to go in search of tissues or toilet paper, the former of which he found on the kitchen counter, next door.

"Sorry," Irene murmured. "I'm sorry, I—"

"There's no need to apologise, Mrs Teague."

"If you're able to answer any questions, I need to ask you both about Danielle's life," Sophie continued. "I can also come back another time."

"No, *no*," Irene almost shouted. "I want to help. I need to help."

Sophie nodded. "We can stop at any time," she said. "But, if you could tell me, first of all, whether Danielle had a boyfriend that you knew of?"

Adam turned to his wife. "Dani would never speak to me about any of that," he said. "What about you, love?"

Irene ran a hand over her face, trying to stay focused while her mind processed the shock. "She—I—no, I don't think so," she replied. "I think she might have had a few casual partners, but nobody she described as a boyfriend."

"All right," Sophie said. "What about her plans after the summer? Do you know what she was planning to do?"

"She said she wanted to go to London, although, with what money, I don't know."

"She never spoke to you about anyone else, or anyone special?"

Both of them shook their heads. "We didn't see enough of her," Irene whispered. "I'll never forgive myself."

"This isn't your fault, Mrs Teague," Sophie said. "It may not be anybody's fault, but, if it is, we'll find them."

"Thank you," Adam said. "Can we see her? Can we see Danielle?"

Sophie understood the need, despite not being a parent herself, but she knew that some things, once seen, could never be unseen.

"I think you should give us time to look after her," she said gently. "You can come to see her at the mortuary tomorrow; one of my team will be in touch with you to arrange it."

"What if the identification was wrong?" Irene said. "That's possible, isn't it?"

Not in this case, Sophie thought.

"I don't want you to harbour any false hopes, Mrs Teague. Danielle has passed away."

She reached down and placed a card on their coffee table, containing various numbers including a good counsellor.

"If you think of anything else, you can call me at any time," she said, and then rose to her feet.

Turner did the same, and they left Danielle's parents to their grief.

CHAPTER 30

Isolde ended the call to her producer, and looked over to find Tristan had woken up.

He said nothing, asked nothing, and demanded nothing.

“That was my producer, back at Channel One,” she said.

“I heard,” he replied.

“They—he wants me back, as soon as possible,” she said, and rose from her chair to begin pacing around the room. “Their ratings are down, and they need me to get back to work, if I’m well enough.”

Tristan was feeling much better himself, so he swung his legs out of the bed.

"Be careful," she said.

"As much as I've enjoyed having you as my nurse, I can't milk this any longer," he said, with the ghost of a smile. "Besides, you were about to tell me that you're leaving soon. Is that right?"

Isolde felt a lump rise in her throat, but she nodded. "I've worked so hard for my career, Tristan, and I love my job. I can't abandon it, now."

He took her hands in his own, and kissed each one in turn. "You don't have to," he said. "I would never ask it of you."

She let out a tremulous breath. "I don't know how this is going to work, otherwise," she said. "And—and, I know you don't agree with me, but this has all happened too fast. Neither of us can really be sure of anything, can we?"

He said nothing at first, but gave her a smile that was tinged with sadness. "You have to do what is best for you," he said, and let go of her hands to begin picking up his clothes. "If you need time, you should take all that you need."

She watched him move around the room, and was torn between two worlds. "When would I see you again?"

"I can come over to visit you," he said. "There are some things to tie up here, first, anyway. The funerals, the investigation, not to mention the mess my uncle left behind."

"I could stay—"

"No," he said, with a small shake of his head. "You were right, Isolde. We both knew this weekend couldn't last, and we have to be realistic. I have work here and in New York, and you have your life and your work in Dublin. I can come over and visit you soon, if you like—and we can see where things stand."

It should have felt like a solution, but instead it felt like an ending.

She lifted her chin. "That sounds fine," she said brightly. "It's the best thing for both of us."

His face was averted, as he tugged on a pair of jeans. "Yes, absolutely."

When Tristan and Isolde emerged downstairs, it was to find the hotel overrun with police.

"What's happened now?" Tristan asked.

"They're searching for the padlock key," Luke said, walking over to join them. "Glad to see you back on your feet again."

"Thanks," he replied, and turned briefly to Isolde. "You and your brother have some catching up to do, so I'll leave you to it. See you later."

He pressed a kiss to her cheek, and then moved off to thank his staff for their service the night before.

"Will you be all right?" she called over.

Tristan stopped, and then turned back, his face shadowed in the light of the terrace doors. "I'll survive," he said. "After this weekend, I can survive anything."

When he moved off again, Luke turned to his sister. "What did he mean when he said we have catching up to do?"

Isolde watched Tristan disappear around the corner, and felt her heart stutter. "Ah—oh, I heard from my producer," she explained. "Owen wants me to come back as soon as possible."

"Is that a good idea?" Luke asked. "You were so unwell, when you arrived on Friday. It's only been a couple of days."

"Yes, but so much has happened," she said. "I haven't been unwell while I've been here, which probably means it was just a blip. Besides..." She lifted her hands. "I need some time to think and be sure of my own feelings," she said. "Everything has happened so quickly, I don't want to make any big life decisions while I'm still reeling from what's happened."

Luke nodded. "That sounds wise, so what's the problem? Has Tristan tried to talk you out of it?"

"No," she said, and realised she was disappointed about that. "He didn't try to talk me out of leaving, at all."

"Perhaps because he knows it's the right thing for you," Luke said.

"Maybe." She hunched down and began to stroke the downy fur on Madge's head. "What would you do, eh?" she asked.

"Madge would do what's right for her, and her alone," her brother said. "Out of sight isn't always out of mind, Isolde."

She looked up at him and nodded. "I hope so."

Tristan found a quiet spot on the terrace and sat down, watching the police shuffle around the shrubbery and poke in the bins with a detachment he was certain he wouldn't have felt a few days ago.

"Penny for them."

He looked up to find Gabi standing there, and smiled.

"I'm not sure they're worth a penny," he replied.

"Can I join you?"

"Of course."

She pulled up a seat beside him, and raised her face to the sunshine. "This is more like it," she said. "How are you doing?"

He supposed she meant physically. "Much better now—thanks for all your help, last night."

"Our pleasure," she said. "But I was wondering how you're doing now that Isolde is going to be leaving."

He looked across at her, and thought that news travelled fast. "You heard, eh?"

She nodded.

"I'm happy for her," he said, and slipped on a pair of sunglasses to shield his eyes from the sun and her penetrating gaze. "Isolde has everything waiting for her in Dublin, so she needs to get back to it."

"And what about the two of you?"

"I can visit," he said, but knew in his heart that it wasn't a long-term solution.

"Don't you think—"

"Look," he said softly. "She needs to go, and I have to stay here for now. I can't argue with her, because you can't force people to feel things they don't feel, and I wouldn't want to. If she isn't sure of herself, she should wait until she is and take the time and space to think about it. I can be patient."

Gabi put a hand on his arm. "She does feel the same, you know. She just doesn't trust herself."

"Perhaps it's me she doesn't trust."

Gabi shook her head. "Give her time," she said, and then put a hand to her head as a sudden spasm of pain caught her by surprise. "Sorry, I've had a headache on and off, all morning."

"Do you need anything?"

"I've taken all the painkillers I can," she said. "It must be dehydration or something."

"I'll fetch you some water," he offered, and began to get up.

Before she could reply, they heard one of the police officers shouting across the terrace to Sophie, who'd been conferring with the constables searching the garden area.

"Boss! We've found something!"

They watched Sophie run across the lawn, and Tristan sank back against his chair with a sigh. He should have felt relief or some sort of elation, because, if they'd found the key to the tunnel's padlock, it increased the chances that they might also find his uncle's fingerprints on it and that would be enough to close the matter. Instead, he felt a terrible emptiness in the pit of his stomach, and an ache in the region of his heart.

CHAPTER 31

Sophie studied the ornate iron key that had been placed into an evidence bag by the forensics team, and wondered what secrets it might hold.

"This looks about the right size," she said. "You can access the tunnel through the panelling under the stairs there, and check to see if it's the right key."

The senior Scenes of Crimes officer, a man by the name of Irwin, rustled in his polypropylene suit, feeling uncomfortably hot.

"We'll get it swabbed and printed as soon as possible," he said.

"How soon is 'soon'?"

"It's a Sunday," he said, in a tone that told her clearly she was lucky he'd even turned up. "We can't work miracles, you know."

"I've seen you work plenty," she said, buttering him up a bit. "The truth is, I'm particularly interested in knowing whether one person's prints are on this key."

"Who? I can take some prints while I'm here and compare them at the lab."

"They're not here," she said. "They're lying on a slab at the mortuary in Truro."

"The other victim?" he said. "Intriguing."

"I'm not sure whether he was a victim or a perpetrator, but it's looking to be the latter. If we find his prints on that key, we'll have an answer."

Irwin was a jobsworth in many ways, but he had a nose for detection. "I could run down there, on my way home," he said.

"You could."

"And if I did?"

"You'd find a pair of tickets to the theatre waiting in your pigeonhole tomorrow morning, as a thank you from me."

Bribery and corruption was not the way to get ahead, as Sophie would say until her dying day.

However, when it came to pushing an investigation to its conclusion, an incentive here and there never hurt anybody.

"Where did you find the key, anyway?"

"It was hidden in plain sight," Irwin replied. "The metal is so aged it's almost completely brown, so it blends in with the colour of the wood in that cleaning cupboard beneath the stairs. Somebody over the years must have hollowed out a little slot for it in the woodwork, and slipped it inside. It was almost invisible to the naked eye; we only found it because we were doing a fingertip search."

He might have been an avaricious old git, she thought, but he did a thorough job.

"It's a pity they moved Williams' body so quickly," Irwin happened to say. "We could have taken his prints more easily, if he was here."

He shuffled back to his work, leaving Sophie to think of a new idea.

Mark Williams was no longer at the hotel, but Danielle Teague was, for the coroner had to travel some distance to get there and had run into storm damage on the road which had delayed their journey. When she'd gone through the woman's personal effects, she hadn't only found the scrap of a note, but also a smartphone that was soaked with water. Without much hope of its recovery, she had taken out the battery and placed it in a bowl of rice, which was supposed to draw out the water and bring the little electronic device back to life. It occurred to Sophie that, if the process worked, she might be able to access the content on Danielle's phone using the girl's own fingerprint—including her banking records.

It was a grisly thought, but it might just work.

In the end, it did work.

The bowlful of rice had drawn out the water in Danielle's smartphone sufficiently to allow Sophie to turn it on again, albeit with a distorted screen and a general feeling that it would give out at any moment. That being the case, she steeled herself to face death once again, and retrieved the key for the cold storage unit off the hotel's kitchens.

"Boss?"

She almost leapt from her skin. "Turner! How many times have I told you not to sneak about like that?"

He folded his arms. "Sorry, I'll warn you the next time," he quipped. "What are you doing?"

"Never you mind."

"It looks like you're trying to access the dead girl's phone using her fingerprint or facial ID."

"That would be highly unprofessional," she said, with a glint. "And I'll thank you not to suggest it."

"You want me to keep watch?"

"About time."

Turner grinned.

"It's not technically against the law," she reasoned. "And it might give us some answers without having to go through the rigmarole of requesting records from the bank or her e-mail service provider. If we can get this thing to open, she probably has everything on an app."

"What do you expect to find?"

"Regular deposits in cash," Sophie said. "Or one large one. It would tally with Tristan's story about his uncle having been blackmailed by her."

"Dangerous game," Turner remarked.

Sophie opened the door to the storage room, pulled a face, and then dipped inside.

A moment later, she hurried out again.

"The fingertip worked," she said, simply. "We're in."

Meg found her son in the library, and, for a moment, she thought it might have been his father standing there, thirty years earlier. They were of a similar height, and she could still remember the first time she'd met a young Harry Williams at one of the youth dances in Newquay. He'd swept her off her feet, quite literally, and set the bar for a long and happy life together.

It was all she ever wanted for their son, too.

"Tristan?"

He turned and smiled at her. "Hello, Mum. You should be resting—you've had a long night."

It was the mark of the man she'd raised that he was more concerned with her wellbeing than his own, despite all he had endured.

"I wanted to see you," she said, and wheeled herself in. "Where's Isolde?"

"I think she's speaking to her brother," he said. "She might be packing."

"Packing? What for?"

"She's going home, across the sea back to Ireland."

Meg heard everything he was trying not to say, and her heart broke for him. "She has her work, and her life there."

"Yes."

"What are you going to do about it?"

"There's nothing I can do about it, at the moment. We have funerals to arrange and all kinds of other things, before I can leave here. They're expecting me back in New York on Wednesday."

"Who's 'they'?"

"The board," he replied.

She nodded, and folded her hands. "And who's head of the board?"

Tristan sighed. "It isn't that simple," he said. "She needs space."

Meg nodded, thinking carefully about the woman she'd come to know. "From what she's told me, Isolde didn't have what you had, growing up," she said. "She doesn't know what it means to have happy parents who love one another, so she finds it hard to imagine that kind of life for herself. That doesn't mean she doesn't want it. If you'll listen to your old mum, I'd tell you to give her space, but not for too long."

Tristan leaned down to kiss his mother's head. "I know what this is really about," he said.

"What's that?"

"Grandchildren. You've been hinting for years."

"That's entirely beside the point," she sniffed.

CHAPTER 32

By the end of the day, Sophie had reinforced one of the greatest rules of murder detection, which is that the silent witnesses to any crime often held the answers. In the case of Danielle Teague, her fingerprint gave access to her smartphone, which, in turn, allowed them to see her online banking app. Her recent transactions showed regular cash deposits of hundreds of pounds, which far exceeded her usual income and could not be accounted for by any other means. To be doubly sure, Sophie planned to check the amounts against any withdrawals made by the late Mark Williams, although that would have to wait until regular working hours. In the meantime, she had the comfort of knowing that none of those amounts were withdrawn by any of the other people who had known Danielle, including Tristan and Simon Anstell, both of whom had voluntarily submitted their banking details for her perusal.

They would never be able to say exactly how Danielle came to die, but the closer Sophie came to corroborating Tristan's version of events, the more she could rely upon his statement that Mark Williams was responsible and had admitted as much before he died.

As for Mark Williams, he, too, had been a silent witness to his own actions. Irwin was true to his word, and made a detour on his way home to the mortuary at Truro Hospital, where he took copies of Williams' fingerprints and compared them with the slides he had recovered from the key. Though there were no full prints to be found, there were several partial matches, all of whom belonged to the dead man.

"I'll tie up any loose ends this week," Sophie said to the small crowd, who had gathered in the ballroom for old time's sake. "But, for now, I'm satisfied that we can close the investigation.

There is no feasible explanation for Mark's prints to have been on that key, if he hadn't been using it, which is something he expressly denied and which we all heard."

There were nods around the table.

"What about Danielle?" Isolde asked.

"My best working theory is that Mark lured her into the tunnel after leaving a note, ostensibly written by Tristan," Sophie said. "The forensics team found minor blood spatter in the cleaning cupboard which I expect to match up with her DNA, or Tristan's, or both. He knocked them out first, coming at them from behind with a hard implement, and then dragged them the rest of the way to the gate, where he left both Danielle and Tristan to drown in the tide with access to safety barred and nobody to hear them shout."

"Evil man," Meg said, with feeling. "Harry will be turning in his grave."

"We know that Danielle was receiving regular cash sums, which dried up in the past week or so. We'll check his accounts, but it's safe to assume for now that these sums had been paid by Mark up until then. When he stopped, she threatened to tell his nephew all about his business dealings, and Mark took action to prevent that happening. When he realised she had already alerted Tristan to something being the matter, he decided to deal with Tristan, too, with the added benefit of making it look like he had some involvement in Danielle's death."

"Is it all over, then?" Tristan asked her.

Sophie nodded. "There'll be a bit of bureaucracy to deal with, I'm afraid," she said, and reached for a glass of water. "Sorry, I've had a headache all day."

Tristan frowned, thinking that there was something he should know that was just out of reach.

It was probably nothing.

Isolde had just finished packing when there came a knock at her door.

"Meg," she said. "Come in." She stepped aside to allow the lady to enter, which she did, with slow and careful movements.

"I'm tired today," Meg explained. "I don't think any of us managed too much sleep last night, did we?"

Isolde could only shake her head.

"Can I get you anything? Something to drink?"

"No, dear, I'm fine. I came to see you because Tristan told me you're going away, tomorrow."

Isolde nodded. "I think it's for the best, for now at least."

"I understand completely," Meg said. "I'm not here to talk you out of anything; I'm here to offer you an ear, if you need it, and pass on an invitation."

"An invitation?"

"To dinner," she said. "Tristan requests the pleasure of your company in the library, at seven."

Isolde smiled beautifully. "I'd be delighted."

"I'll go and tell him—"

"Wait, Meg. Can I ask you a question?"

"Anything you like."

"How did you know, when you met Tristan's father, that he was the right one for you?"

Meg wheeled herself a bit closer and tapped one of the bedroom chairs, indicating that Isolde should sit beside her.

"You never know," she said simply, when Isolde came beside her. "There isn't any divine hand that taps you on the shoulder and tells you a person is the one you should make a life with. In my experience, you meet somebody who makes you feel everything you haven't felt before, and they may not be perfect—in fact, they won't be. But you're both imperfect, and you make an imperfect life together that's absolutely perfect for the both of you. It takes constant work and effort, and a lot of love. You expect to argue and make mistakes, and be angry sometimes, but never so angry that it outweighs all that's good. You live a happy life because you both care for the other person more than you care about yourself, and that's how you know you're with the right one."

Isolde let her words sink in, and then nodded. "Thank you, Meg."

"Anytime, dear."

When Isolde went downstairs just before seven, she found the library decked in candles and, this time, not because of any power outage. A single table for two had been set out, and Tristan came to his feet as she entered the room.

"I thought a farewell dinner was in order," he said, and offered her a glass of champagne. "You look beautiful."

"Thank you," she replied, and clinked her glass with his. "This was a lovely thought."

"It's the least I could do, for the woman who saved my life twice in one day."

She smiled. "I think we're even on that score; don't forget, you fought off your uncle on the bridge."

"Well, who's counting, anyway?"

They sat down, and their first course arrived shortly after. When they were alone again, he smiled at her across the table. "It's been quite the weekend, hasn't it?"

"That's putting it mildly," she agreed. "How does it feel to be cleared as the prime suspect?"

"Anticlimactic," he said, with a laugh. "I hardly had any time at all to develop my infamy."

"Well, you're still young. There's still time."

He smiled, and sat back to look at her. "Isolde, I know you're leaving in the morning, and we can figure things out from there," he said. "But we still have this evening, and I never managed to steal a dance from you."

She rested her head on her hand. "No, you didn't. We were interrupted."

"It doesn't seem fair, does it?" He took out his phone and fiddled with the music system playing around their heads, changing it from the ubiquitous classical background to Neil Young singing about a Harvest Moon. "Will you?"

He held out a hand, and they moved around the room together, their bodies entwined, saying nothing until the song ended and another began.

"Tristan?"

"Mm?"

"If I asked you to come and stay with me in Dublin, would you?"

He stopped moving, and stepped back to look into her eyes. "I've already said, I'll visit you whenever you like."

"No, I mean…if we wanted to really try to make a go of things. Would you consider it?"

He thought of his life in New York, and his mother's words swam back into his mind. He was the head of the company, and they had hotels all around the world, including in Dublin. It was far easier for him to live there than for Isolde to try to relocate her work, so the decision was an easy one. The only thing that prevented him from thinking of it earlier or suggesting it to her was his concern that his feelings outweighed hers, and a desire not to create any pressure.

But now it was she who was suggesting that they make the leap, and his heart responded.

"Of course, I would," he said. "I'm a risk-taker, as you know."

She grinned. "And I suppose I'm a risky prospect?"

"Are you kidding?" he said, pulling her into his arms again. "You've been nothing but trouble, since we met."

"I could say the same."

"We're well matched, then, wouldn't you say?"

"Imperfectly perfect," she whispered.

"What's that?"

"Oh, nothing. Just something your mother said."

The soft strains of Van Morrison's *Into the Mystic* began to play, and he spun her around to make her laugh.

"I just remembered something else," he said.

"What's that? And you'd better not say that you're married."

"Not yet," he said, enigmatically. "I was actually just thinking that you owe me quite a number of personal, one-to-one sessions."

"Ah, yes, the public relations coaching," she said.

"I think it might be more beneficial to cover all aspects of interpersonal relationship building," he said, while his voice was muffled against her hair.

"Where do you suggest we start?"

He looked into her eyes, and smiled. "Here," he said, and kissed her deeply.

CHAPTER 33

Monday morning

The next morning marked a departure for most of the residents of the Tintagel Hotel, including Isolde, her brother and his wife, as well as Sophie and Gabriel. The latter were the first to leave, on account of her needing to drive back to St Ives and, in her own words, "drag PC Turner's sorry arse out of bed" so they could fight crime for another day. Gabriel had the remainder of his book to write, for which their recent experiences had provided ample inspiration, and the pair of them left with a promise to keep in touch.

Isolde waved them off, having thanked Sophie again for all she'd done, and then turned to the other member of their party who'd been sorely neglected. "Madge." The dog trotted over to where Isolde was seated in the reception hall, and put her head on her lap.

"I'm sorry we didn't get to spend more time together," she murmured, and gave the dog's ears a good scratch. "I'll come and visit you again, soon."

"And what about the rest of us?" Gabi asked.

"If there's one thing I've learned lately, it's that I need to see more of my family," Isolde said. "I'll book my next flight as soon as I get home."

"You'd better," Luke said, coming to sit beside her. "Next time you're not feeling well, or need anything at all, you can call me anytime. I'm always here, Isolde."

She nodded, and hugged him hard. "Thank you," she said. "By the way, Tristan and I have decided to give things a go."

Gabi's face lit up. "You have? Oh, that's wonderful!"

"I decided is life was about taking risks, sometimes," Isolde said. "But I don't think I would've had the courage, if I hadn't seen how happy you both are."

"Name your firstborn after me, and we'll call it even," Luke said.

"Har har."

Tristan joined them then, jangling a set of car keys. "Time to go, if you don't want to be late for your flight," he said, and Isolde nodded, turning to her brother and sister-in-law. "I'll miss you."

"And we'll miss you," Gabi said. "I'm sorry I drank all your tea."

Isolde laughed. "There's more where that came from, I'm sure," she said.

"If it's any consolation, I gave myself a stomach-ache," Gabi replied. "It's probably all the ginger or lemongrass, or something."

They made their farewells, and then, while Tristan took her bag to the car, Isolde went in search of Meg. She found her in her usual place, beside the window in the library, reading a copy of *Wuthering Heights.*

"Meg? I'm leaving now."

She set her book down, and opened her arms to the woman her son loved, and whom she was learning to love, too. "Take care," she said. "And good luck to both of you. Come and visit me again, soon."

"Tristan can't join me for another week," Isolde said. "But, once we're settled, I'm going to make sure one of the bedrooms is made properly accessible for you, Meg. I hope you'll visit Ireland as often as you like."

Meg patted her cheek, as she would have done her own daughter.

"You're a kind person, Isolde. My son's a lucky man."

"We're both lucky."

Isolde kissed her cheek and moved off with a wave. Once she was out of view, Meg rubbed her hands together with the kind of unbridled glee that could only be produced by a grandmother-in-waiting.

Tristan drove Isolde to the airport but, rather than leaving with a heavy heart, as he'd imagined, they parted with the excitement of a next chapter being just around the corner. He had matters to attend to in Tintagel, as well as in New York, but he planned to join her in Dublin a week from then. In the meantime, Isolde would return to work and to Maeve, who would be surprised but, hopefully, very happy for her. There would need to be some changes to their living arrangements in due course, but there was no reason why the three of them couldn't live happily together in the interim, especially as Tristan would be travelling for at least a week out of every month on business. They'd talked it all out, and all that remained was to look forward to a bright new future together.

Isolde thought about all this and more as she paid off Mad Andy's taxi, and paused to look up at her townhouse. The last time she'd been there, she'd been eager to leave it and the memories behind. Now, she looked at her home with renewed vision, in more ways than one. It had been a happy place for a long time, and no single incident could outweigh that. Whoever had invaded her space was long gone, now, and the memory of it was behind her, superseded by all that had happened since.

She slotted her key into the lock, and stepped inside.

Upstairs, she heard the sound of a hairdryer, and decided to surprise her friend. Isolde tiptoed upstairs and along to Maeve's bedroom door, which was ajar. Smiling to herself, she raised a hand to push open the door.

"*Surprise!*"

Maeve shrieked, and dropped the hairdryer. In the seconds it took for her to retrieve it, Isolde noticed that her friend had changed the colour and style of her hair, so that it was now a long, honey blonde.

Like her own.

There were many women who chose to colour their hair in that way, and in that style, but it was a surprise to find Maeve had gone for such a shift. Nonetheless, it suited her, and she thought no more about it.

"Isolde?" she said. "You scared the living daylights out of me!" Maeve rose to her feet, and Isolde noticed she was wearing a pair of her trousers and one of her cream blouses. Still, that wasn't an issue, because they often borrowed one another's clothing.

Like sisters.

"I like your outfit," she joked. "I'll have to put a lock on my wardrobe door next time I'm gone!"

Maeve didn't laugh, but was defensive. "I needed an outfit, since I've been covering your slot while you were away," she said, testily.

Isolde held up a hand. "I'm only kidding! You know you're welcome to borrow anything of mine."

"Why are you back so early?" Maeve asked. "I thought you were planning to stay for a few weeks in Cornwall?"

Isolde winced, and mentally cursed Owen for failing to impart the news to her friend. "Ah, well, I heard from Owen while I was away," she said. "He asked me to come back as soon as possible, so I came back in time to present the evening news tonight."

Maeve set down the hairbrush she was holding. "You were ill," she said. "Wasn't he the one who sent you packing?"

"I wouldn't quite put it like *that*," Isolde said, with a laugh. "He suggested I take a sabbatical but, in the end, I only needed a few days to feel much better. You know, I haven't had a single headache, stomach cramp or any blurred vision since I've been away? It must be all the sea air!"

Maeve smiled. "That must be it."

"You won't believe it when I tell you everything that's happened," Isolde continued. "You couldn't make it up."

"Try me."

Isolde chattered happily about brushes with death, storms and then, finally, about Tristan. "I think you'll really like him, Maeve."

"I'll have to, won't I? So long as he's kind to my friend, then he'll be alright in my book," she said, with a smile. "When is he coming over?"

"In a week," Isolde said, and turned to her with a pained expression. "I know it's short notice, and I don't want you to worry about anything changing around here. He can always stay at his hotel, if things get too much, and we find we need our space. It'll be a big adjustment for all of us."

"Isn't it all a bit…quick?" Maeve asked, gently.

"I know, it seems that way," Isolde said. "But sometimes you have to just go with it. If it doesn't work out, at least we can say we tried."

Maeve raised an eyebrow. "Who are you, and what have you done with Isolde?"

She laughed, and then made a small exclamation at the time. "Oops! I'd better start getting changed out of these travel clothes," she said. "I need to be at the station in an hour."

Maeve watched her skip out of the room, blonde hair swishing at her back, and sank down onto her dressing room stool. She stared at herself in the mirror for long minutes, noticing the subtle differences in her hair and Isolde's, with her own being considerably less natural looking. There was an angularity to her face that wasn't present in Isolde's, and the blouse she wore didn't fit her quite as well as it did its real owner. Very slowly, and very deliberately, she began to rip it off, sending the row of neatly sewn buttons flying onto the floor.

CHAPTER 34

When Tristan returned to the Tintagel Hotel, he was surprised to find Luke and Gabi's car still parked in the car park, and the man himself still seated in the reception area.

"I thought you'd both be gone, by now," he said.

"So did I," Luke said. "Gabi isn't well."

"I'm sorry to hear it," Tristan said. "Anything I can do?"

"I don't think so; she's been having dreadful headaches and cramps, and she said her vision was blurring a bit."

Something niggled at the back of Tristan's mind. "Sophie was complaining of headaches," he said, and then an awful, sinking feeling began to settle in the pit of his stomach.

"When did Gabi start feeling this way?" he asked.

Luke thought about it. "She had a headache late Saturday morning, but she said that was to do with the cocktails from the night before."

"I don't remember her having too many," Tristan said.

"Come to think of it...you're right."

"What did Gabi eat for breakfast on Saturday?"

Luke shrugged. "We were out on the terrace with Isolde," he remembered. "She had the Full Cornish—which reminds me to warn you about my sister's voracious appetite—"

"Noted, thank you."

"—I had a bacon sandwich and Gabi had some cereal."

"What about drinks?"

"I had a coffee, Gabi and Isolde had some of that God-awful herbal tea."

Tristan's heart began to pound. "Gabi was drinking that tea yesterday, as well," he said. "When you were making sandwiches on the barbeque, she was boiling a big pot of water to make teas and coffees for everyone. I saw her drinking it, and I think Sophie had some, too."

"And Sophie's been having headaches," Luke murmured, and then sat bolt upright on the sofa. "You think there's something in that tea?"

"I can't help but wonder. Where did Isolde get it?"

Luke went back over the conversations he'd had with his sister, and one name stuck out. "Maeve," he said suddenly. "Isolde didn't get the tea, Maeve did. She said it was a gift from her friend to help her get well again."

"Or the opposite," Tristan said, and took out his phone to begin searching for flights. "Isolde told me she'd been ill for weeks, until she was finally unable to work and had to come here to lick her wounds. Maeve works with Isolde at the channel, doesn't she?"

Luke nodded. "She does the weather."

"Uh-huh. And, what if she wanted to read the news? She'd have no chance, with Isolde on the scene."

Luke ran a worried hand over his face. "We've had a dramatic weekend," he said. "We can't start jumping at shadows around every corner. I'm sure there's a very reasonable explanation."

"She can tell me all about it, when I land in Dublin," Tristan said, and raised the phone to his ear. "There's a flight in two hours, and I'm going to be on it."

"I'll ring Isolde to tell her not to drink any more of that tea," Luke suggested, but then he stopped mid-dial.

Tristan ended his call, and gave him a questioning glance. "What stopped you?"

"If Maeve gave her something to make her ill, deliberately, then she's dangerous," Luke said. "If we call Isolde, she may not be able to hide her feelings, and Maeve will be alerted. We don't know what she might do, or what else she might have in her arsenal."

Tristan nodded, and then another thought occurred to him. "The intruder," he said. "The man who broke in and terrified Isolde before she came here? What if that was all orchestrated to scare her away? Get Gabi to a hospital, and tell Sophie to have whatever's left of that tea checked out by her forensics team," he said. "I'm going back to the airport."

With that, he turned on his heel and strode back out into the sunshine. A moment later, Luke heard the rumble of a car's engine heading along the gravel driveway at speed.

He hurried upstairs to find his wife.

Isolde's return to Channel One was marked by a series of spontaneous hugs, cheers, and kind words from all of the production staff, who welcomed her back on set with genuine delight. For her part, she was ready to take up the helm once again, and gave a flawless performance for her viewing public.

"And now, we'll turn to the weather. Maeve? Can you tell us what to expect this week?"

Maeve painted a brittle smile on her face, and began prattling about wind temperatures and cold snaps.

"Thank you, Maeve! After all the sunshine we've been enjoying, I guess we all needed a little reminder that this is still glorious Ireland, after all, eh?"

Maeve said nothing, but continued to smile brilliantly, and, feeling slightly confused by the lack of byplay, Isolde began to recite her outro.

"That's about all from us, folks," she said. "And, on a personal note, I want to thank all those viewers who wrote in with their well wishes while I was away. I'm pleased to say I'm back to full health, and will be back on your screen for the morning news, tomorrow. Until then, have a lovely evening."

There was a silent countdown, followed by a shout of *CLEAR!* and then a smattering of applause.

"Welcome back," Owen said, coming to join her. "You've got that magic touch, Isolde. Any trouble with your vision?"

"Nope," she said. "It's completely clear."

Maeve wandered across to see them. "That was great as always," she said, with forced cheer. "Listen, to celebrate your return, I thought I could cook us a bit of dinner tonight, what do you say? Like the old days, before we have a man around the house, eh?"

Owen was intrigued. "A man?"

Isolde couldn't keep the smile from her face. "I met someone special, while I was in Cornwall—"

"Not just *anyone*," Maeve cut in, hopping up onto the news desk. "He's the CEO of the Williams Hotel Group."

"*Tristan* Williams?" Owen said.

Isolde was embarrassed, because, in all the time she'd known him, she'd never really thought of Tristan in those terms. She didn't see his labels; she only saw the man himself.

"Yes," she said, coming to her feet. "It's his family's business. He's travelling over in a week to join me, so you'll meet him sometime, I'm sure."

"Does he have a brother?" Maeve joked.

"Sadly not," Isolde grinned, and was pleased to see her friend back to her usual form. "I'll see if he has any friends, though."

CHAPTER 35

The scent of fragrant meat permeated the house and Isolde followed it to the kitchen, where she found her friend stirring red wine into a beef casserole. Music played on the radio in the background, and Maeve jiggled her hips in time to it as she moved between the oven and the counter.

"There you are," she said, as Isolde entered the room. "Were you all right in the bath?"

Isolde had experienced some initial nerves when she'd first gone into her bathroom again, for it was impossible not to remember what had happened there before. But the feeling soon dissipated, and she was able to enjoy soaking in the bath as she'd always done. "It was fine," she said. "Until the scent of this wonderful food drove me out, that is. Can I help with something?"

"Just pour us a couple of glasses of vino tinto," Maeve said, and waggled a nice bottle of Malbec in her general direction. "Tonight, we feast."

She watched Isolde go off in search of a corkscrew, and, while her back was turned, she produced a small bag of what looked like dried herbs. She sprinkled them into the casserole, stuffed the plastic bag back into her pocket, and stirred it all in before Isolde returned.

"Oh, the corkscrew was here, all along," she said, spotting it beside Maeve's hand.

"So it was," she said. "Here you are."

Isolde popped the cork and poured a glass for her friend, then one for herself. Once they'd toasted each other, she slid onto one of the bar stools next to the island.

"We're almost ready here," Maeve said.

"It smells delicious."

"*Bon appetit.*" Maeve placed a steaming bowl of casserole and mashed potatoes in front of Isolde, who would later think that she should have wondered why she'd chosen to serve such a wintry meal in high summer. However, all she saw was the food, the company, and her good friend whom she'd missed.

"Thanks," she said, and took a healthy bite. "It tastes wonderful."

"Eat it all up," Maeve said, and moved her own food around her plate. "You need to keep your strength up."

"Honestly, you don't need to worry about me," Isolde said. "I'm much better, now."

"It's amazing how these things can come on," Maeve murmured.

They chatted about station gossip until Isolde gave a huge, jaw-cracking yawn and propped her head on her hand.

"Sorry, Maeve, I don't know what's come over me," she said. "I feel so tired, all of a sudden."

"That's a pity."

Maeve reached across to clear their plates, and began washing them up with more force than was necessary.

"I think I'm just going to go and sit on the sofa—leave the dishes, and I'll do them," Isolde said, and yawned again.

She staggered off the stool, and saw black spots dance in front of her eyes.

"Go and sit down, Isolde."

"I think I will," she replied, and moved carefully through to the living room, where she collapsed onto the sofa.

A minute or two later, Maeve joined her, and looked down at her as though she were a specimen in a lab.

"Feeling alright?" she wondered.

Isolde felt sick, and her whole body felt incapable of movement.

"I—I don't feel well—"

Maeve snorted, and sat herself on the edge of the coffee table so that she could look at Isolde.

"You had to come back, didn't you?" she whispered. "You couldn't have just stayed away for a few more weeks."

Isolde tried to focus on her friend, but her face was distorted.

"It's always been the same," Maeve continued. "For years and years, now, ever since we were kids in school. It was always, 'Isolde Malone, this' and 'Isolde Malone, that'. *Poor* Isolde, since her parents were divorcing. *Clever* Isolde, for getting all the best grades. *Beautiful* Isolde, with her blonde hair and her baby-blue eyes."

She spat the words like venom.

"You knew it, as well, didn't you? You could have any boy you wanted. You want to go to Trinity College? Sure, right enough, here you go, Isolde. Welcome in, and never mind about your friend, Maeve. She'll manage down the road. What's that, Isolde? You want to be a TV star? No problem, here you are."

Maeve was ranting now, the words coming faster and faster as she let the skeletons fly.

"Well, you're not as clever as they all think, are you, Isolde? You had no idea you were being poisoned, all these weeks. What kind of moron doesn't realise *that*?"

She laughed, and stood up to pace around.

"I didn't even want to kill you," she said. "I only needed you to move over, and give me a chance, for once. Go away, and stay away for a while, so I can have a shot. But *no*. You couldn't do it, could you? You just couldn't stay away."

Isolde listened through a haze, trying to grasp what she was saying, but unable to believe it.

"And then—*then*!—you have the nerve to tell me that you've met someone. And, oh, not just anyone. It wouldn't be Joe Bloggs from over the hill for Isolde Malone, *would it*? It had to be a bloody handsome hotel magnate, didn't it? You couldn't, just for once, be *normal*, could you? Rob sends you his regards, by the way. He quite enjoyed playing the part of a masked intruder."

Maeve was on a roll now, too far gone to stop the hatred that was in full flow.

"All these years, you thought I was your friend, didn't you? You honestly thought I wouldn't mind you rubbing it all in my face, every day? Didn't you ever think it would bother me, playing second fiddle?"

Isolde could only stare.

"And then, when you came back into the studio today, when I heard them all clapping at you and cheering..." Maeve said, in disgust. "I could have thrown up. It made me *sick*. You're nothing special, Isolde. In fact, you're nothing at all."

She came back to sit opposite her, suddenly calm again.

"Now, the thing is, what they don't know, and what I'll be telling them, is how much you've been struggling lately. Mentally, you know, after all the drama. You look strong, but aren't looks deceptive? It's always the quiet ones, wouldn't you say? Well, that's what's going to happen to you. You've come home, thinking you're all better—but then you aren't, and you decide to take an overdose. The strain of everything was too much for you, so you wanted to end it all."

Maeve took out several packets of painkillers, and stacked them on the coffee table.

"I'll get you a glass of water," she said, solicitously. "Don't move."

CHAPTER 36

After disembarking the plane, Tristan had run through customs and avoided any long waiting times for baggage, since he hadn't brought any with him. Dublin Airport was around eight miles north of the city centre but was prone to heavy traffic, so he was pleased to find a taxi driver by the name of Andy who defied the laws of physics and man, to get him across to Isolde's house in what must have been record timing.

The lights were on in the house, and he was about to ring the doorbell, when there came a strangled cry from within.

Isolde.

He moved to the window, but could see nothing.

Tristan ran around to the back of the house where, through a chink in the blinds, he could see Isolde sprawled on a sofa with a woman pinning her down, trying to force something down her throat.

Like lightning, he planted his boot in the back door, and, with a couple of hard kicks, it burst open.

"Isolde!"

The other woman, who he assumed was Maeve, ran into the kitchen.

She looked at him, and then snatched up one of the carving knives from the block on the island counter. He barely had time to react before she came at him, swiping wildly with the blade.

He moved quickly, dancing out of reach, jumping back as she continued to stab at the air.

"Come to the rescue again?" she jibed. "You're too late, lover boy. This time, you'll be *too late*."

She made to swipe at him again, but this time he grabbed one of the kitchen stools and used it to fend her off, pinning her into a corner like a wild animal.

All the while, he thought of Isolde.

"What did you give her?" he snarled. "What have you done?"

"It'll make her go away," Maeve said, and began to laugh until tears ran down her face.

The knife clattered to the floor, and he kicked it out of reach. He couldn't pin her there forever, and he was more concerned to find out how Isolde was doing, so he abandoned her in the kitchen and ran through to the living room to find Isolde had passed out, and her heart rate was thready.

He took out a mobile phone to ring for an ambulance, and had barely given them the address when Maeve followed him into the room, knife in hand again.

He dropped the phone and raised his arms to defend himself, taking some deep slashes to his forearms. She tried to lunge at Isolde, but he wrestled with her, tearing the knife from her hands to hurl it across the room, where it spun against the wooden floor and slid beneath a sofa. Then, he pinned her down, and put a knee in her back to keep her there.

"You're early," she said. "You weren't supposed to be here for another week."

Maeve began to laugh again.

The ambulance arrived within minutes, and Isolde was transferred to hospital to have her stomach pumped. Fortunately, Maeve hadn't had the opportunity to force enough pills down Isolde's throat for it to be fatal, however it was likely she would feel unwell for a few days. It was also lucky that the toxins were expelled from her body quickly, for it reduced the likelihood of any serious organ damage. As for Tristan, his knife wounds were bandaged, and he waited in one of the big, wipe-clean hospital chairs beside Isolde's bed until she woke up.

When she did, he smiled.

"Hello," he said.

"Hello," she croaked. "What happened?"

He told her, and she grieved for the friend she'd never had.

"I never knew how much she hated me." Tears pooled in her eyes. "I loved her."

"Maeve's very unwell," Tristan said, as charitably as he could. "Hopefully, the courts will decide to detain her in a mental health facility, because she needs the help."

"I don't know how I was so blind."

"Because you don't walk through life thinking badly of people," he said, and took her hand in his. "It's one of many reasons to love you."

"How did you know?" she asked him. "I wasn't expecting you for another week."

"The tea," he explained. "Gabi was very ill, when I got back to the hotel, and it reminded me that she and Sophie had both suffered from headaches and cramps whenever they'd drunk some of that tea. Luke told me it was Maeve who gave it to you."

Isolde nodded. "Maeve watched me drink it every morning, and every night," she said. "What kind of person could do that?"

"Don't think about it, now," he said.

Isolde closed her eyes, feeling tired again. "You know what this means, don't you?"

"What, my love?"

"It means that you're one up on me, now. You've saved my life three times, whereas I've only saved yours twice."

He laughed. "You can give me a note with an 'IOU'," he said. "In case I ever need to call upon your lifesaving expertise over the course of the next fifty to sixty years."

"That's a long time," she said.

"It'll go by in a flash," he murmured. "So, I was thinking, how about we round off our madcap weekend with another impulsive decision?"

"What did you have in mind?"

"I was thinking of a wedding, actually."

"Oh? Who's the lucky lady?"

He smiled. "I happen to know a good hotel venue, for a reception," he said.

Isolde looked at him, then at her hand, and coughed delicately. "I don't see a ring, mister."

Tristan grinned, and then looked around the room for inspiration. A vase of roses sat on her bedside table, which he'd ordered from a local florist, and he took one of the buds, poking a hole in the middle for her finger.

"It'll have to be a flower ring, for now," he said. "Now, Isolde Malone, will you do me the very great honour of marrying me?"

She looked at the flower on her finger, then at him. "Aye, go on then. So long as we can have an Irish band at the wedding."

"Of course."

"And fish chowder and soda bread."

"Naturally."

"And children," she said softly. "I'd like to have children one day, if we can."

He smiled all the way to his eyes. "Anything else?"

"That's all, for now."

"Isolde?"

"Mm hmm?"

"Is this projection?"

"Nope, this is being in love." She fell asleep smiling, and he stayed with her throughout the night, as he did all the nights for the rest of their lives.

AUTHOR'S NOTE

The idea for *The Haven* came very much from the magical, real-life setting of Tintagel, with its castle, waterfall, beaches, caves, and, of course, its legends. It is truly a special part of the world, and I would always encourage any of my readers to visit and enjoy it if you should ever have the chance.

Now, a note on logistics. Whilst every effort has been made to represent the landscape and geography as accurately as possible, I'm sure you appreciate that in order to tell a good, pacy story, one must sometimes bend the rules. In this instance, I created Williams Cave, which does not exist, nor does its tunnel leading to the Tintagel Hotel—which also doesn't exist. There are, of course, a number of good hotels in the area, and one larger one in particular, but rest assured its setting provided inspiration only, and, as far as I am aware, it is not run by any nefarious characters!

Cornwall is like a second home to me and my family, and my parents lived there for eight happy years. It is always a pleasure to write about its beauty spots, and weave stories around the communities and histories of the area. I hope you enjoyed reading this latest outing of the Summer Suspense gang, and I look forward to introducing you to many more characters in the summers to come.

LJ ROSS
June 2024

ABOUT THE AUTHOR

LJ Ross is an international bestselling author, best known for creating atmospheric mystery and thriller novels, including the DCI Ryan series of Northumbrian murder mysteries which have sold over ten million copies worldwide.

Her debut, *Holy Island*, was released in January 2015 and reached number one in the UK and Australian charts. Since then, she has released more than twenty further novels, all of which have been top three global bestsellers and almost all of which have been UK #1 bestsellers. Louise has garnered an army of loyal readers through her storytelling and, thanks to them, many of her books reached the coveted #1 spot whilst only available to pre-order ahead of release.

Louise was born in Northumberland, England. She studied undergraduate and postgraduate Law at King's College, University of London and then abroad in Paris and Florence. She spent much of her working life in London, where she was a lawyer for a number of years until taking the decision to change career and pursue her dream to write. Now, she writes full time and lives with family in Northumberland.

If you enjoyed *The Haven*, please consider leaving a review online.

If you would like to be kept up to date with new releases from LJ Ross, please complete an e-mail contact form on her Facebook page or website, www.ljrossauthor.com

Scan the QR code below to find out more about LJ Ross and her books

If you enjoyed *The Bay*, why not try the bestselling DCI Ryan Mysteries by LJ Ross?

HOLY ISLAND

A DCI RYAN MYSTERY (Book #1)

Detective Chief Inspector Ryan retreats to Holy Island seeking sanctuary when he is forced to take sabbatical leave from his duties as a homicide detective. A few days before Christmas, his peace is shattered, and he is thrust back into the murky world of murder when a young woman is found dead amongst the ancient ruins of the nearby Priory.

When former local girl Dr Anna Taylor arrives back on the island as a police consultant, old memories swim to the surface making her confront her difficult past. She and Ryan struggle to work together to hunt a killer who hides in plain sight, while pagan ritual and small-town politics muddy the waters of their investigation.

Murder and mystery are peppered with a sprinkling of romance and humour in this fast-paced crime whodunnit set on the spectacular Northumbrian island of Lindisfarne, cut off from the English mainland by a tidal causeway.

If you like DCI Ryan, why not try the bestselling Alexander Gregory Thrillers by LJ Ross?

IMPOSTOR

AN ALEXANDER GREGORY THRILLER (Book #1)

If you like DCI Ryan, why not try the bestselling Alexander Gregory Thrillers by LJ Ross?

IMPOSTOR

AN ALEXANDER GREGORY THRILLER (Book #1)

Keep reading for an extract...

IMPOSTOR

AN ALEXANDER GREGORY THRILLER

LJ ROSS

PROLOGUE

August 1987

She was muttering again.

The boy heard it from beneath the covers of his bed; an endless, droning sound, like flies swarming a body. The whispering white noise of madness.

Poor, poor baby, she was saying. *My poor, poor baby.*

Over and over she repeated the words, as her feet paced the hallway outside his room. The floorboards creaked as she moved back and forth, until her footsteps came to an abrupt halt.

He hunkered further down, wrapping his arms around his legs, as if the pattern of Jedi knights on his *Star Wars* duvet cover could protect him.

It couldn't.

The door swung open and his mother was silhouetted in its frame, fully dressed despite it being the middle of the night. She strode across the room and shook his coiled body with an unsteady hand.

"Wake up! We need to go to the hospital."

The boy tried not to sigh. She didn't like it when he sighed, when he looked at her the 'wrong' way, or when he argued. Even if he did, she wouldn't listen.

She wouldn't even *hear.*

"I'm awake," he mumbled, although his body was crying out for sleep.

He was always sleepy.

"Come on, get dressed," she continued, and he tried not to look directly at her as she scurried about the room, pulling out clothes at random for him to wear. He didn't want to see her eyes, or what was hidden behind them. They'd be dark again, like they were before, and they'd look straight through him.

There came a soft moan from the bedroom next door, and his mother hurried out, leaving him to pull on jeans and a faded *Power Rangers* t-shirt. The clock on the bedside table told him it was three-seventeen a.m., in cheerful neon-green light. If he had the energy to spare, he might have wondered whether the children he'd seen playing in the garden next door ever got sick, like he did, or whether they got to go to school.

He remembered going to school, once.

He remembered liking it.

But his mother said he was too ill to go to school now, and he'd learn so much more at home, where she could take care of him and Christopher.

It wasn't her fault that, despite all her care, neither boy seemed to get any better.

Once, when she thought he was asleep, she'd come in to sit on the edge of his bed. She'd stroked a hand over his hair and told him that she loved him. For a moment, he thought Mummy had come back; but then, she'd moved her mouth close to his ear and told him it was all because Daddy had left them to be with something called a Filthy Whore, and everything would have been alright if he'd never gone away. He hadn't known what she meant. At first, he'd wondered if some kind of galactic monster had lured his father away. Maybe, at this very moment, he was trapped in a cast of bronze, just like Han Solo.

She called his name, and the boy dragged his skinny body off the bed. There was no time to make up fairy tales about his father, or to wonder how other children lived.

Or how they died.

There was more muttering at the hospital.

He could hear it, beyond the turquoise curtain surrounding his hospital bed. Whenever somebody passed by, the material rippled on the wind and he caught sight of the serious-looking doctors and nurses gathered a short distance away.

"*I can't see any medical reason—*" he heard one of them say, before the curtain flapped shut again. "*This needs to be reported.*"

"*There have been cases,*" another argued.

"*One dead already, the youngest in critical condition—*"

The boy tensed as he recognised the quick *slap-slap-slap* of his mother's tread against the linoleum floor.

"Where's my son? Where've you taken him?" she demanded, in a shrill voice. "Is he in there?"

He saw her fingers grasp the edge of the curtain, and unconsciously shrank back against the pillows, but she did not pull it back.

There ensued a short argument, conducted in professional undertones.

"If you really think—alright. Yes, yes, he can stay overnight, so long as I stay with him at all times. But what about Christopher?"

The voices receded back down the corridor as they moved towards the High Dependency Unit, where his younger brother lay against scratchy hospital bedsheets, fighting for his life.

When the boy awoke the next morning, he was not alone.

Three people surrounded his bed. One, he recognised as the doctor who'd snuck him a lollipop the previous night, and she gave him a small smile. Another was a stern-faced man wearing a dark suit that reminded him of his father, and the other was a young woman in a rumpled police uniform with sad brown eyes.

"Hi, there," the doctor said. "How're you doing, champ?"

There was a false note of cheer to her voice that made him nervous.

"W-where's my mum?"

The three adults exchanged an uncomfortable glance.

"You'll see your mother soon," the man told him. "I'm afraid she's had some bad news. You both have."

In careful, neutral tones, they spoke of how his younger brother had died during the night and, with every passing word, the boy's pale, ghostly-white face became more shuttered.

It had happened before, you see.

Last year, his baby sister had died too, before she'd reached her first birthday.

He remembered all the cards and flowers arriving at the house they used to live in; the endless stream of neighbours pouring into his mother's living room to condole and glean a little gossip about their misfortune. He remembered his mother's arm wrapped around his shoulder, cloying and immoveable, like a band of steel.

"*These two are all I have left, now,*" she'd said, tearfully, drawing Christopher tightly against her other side. "*I can only pray that God doesn't take them, too.*"

And, while the mourners tutted and wept and put 'a little something' in envelopes to help out, he'd watched his mother's eyes and wondered why she was so happy.

CHAPTER 1

Ballyfinny, County Mayo, Ireland

Thirty years later

"Daddy, what's an '*eejit*'?"

Liam Kelly exited the roundabout—where he'd recently been cut-up by the aforementioned *eejit* driving a white Range Rover—and rolled his eyes. His three-year-old daughter was growing bigger every day, and apparently her ears were, too.

"That's just a word to describe somebody who… ah, does silly things."

She thought about it.

"Are you an *eejit*, Daddy?"

Liam roared with laughter and smiled in the rear-view mirror.

"It's been said," he admitted, with a wink. "Nearly home now, sugarplum. Shall we tell Mammy all about how well you did in your swimming class, today?"

His daughter grinned and nodded.

"I swam like a fish, didn't I?"

"Aye, you did. Here we are."

It took a minute for him to unbuckle her child seat and to collect their bags, but then Liam and his daughter were skipping hand in hand up the short driveway leading to the front door of their bungalow on the outskirts of the town. It was perched on higher ground overlooking the lough and, though it had been a stretch to buy the place, he was reminded of why they had each time he looked out across the sparkling water.

The front door was open, and they entered the hallway with a clatter of footsteps.

"We're back!" he called out.

But there was not a whisper of sound on the air, and he wondered if his wife was taking a nap. The first trimester was always tiring.

"Maybe Mammy's having a lie-down," he said, and tapped a finger to his lips. "Let's be quiet like mice, alright?"

"Okay," she replied, in a stage whisper.

"You go along and play in your bedroom and I'll bring you a glass of milk in a minute," he said, and smiled as she tiptoed down the corridor with exaggerated care.

When the little girl pushed open the door to her peaches-and-cream bedroom, she didn't notice her mother at first, since she was lying so serenely amongst the stuffed toys on the bed. When she did, she giggled, thinking of the story of Goldilocks.

"You're in my bed!" she whispered.

She crept towards her mother, expecting her eyes to open at any moment.

But they didn't.

The little girl began to feel drowsy after her exertions at the swimming pool, and decided to curl up beside her. She clambered onto the bed and, when her hands brushed her mother's cold skin, she tugged her rainbow blanket over them both.

"That's better," she mumbled, as her eyelids drooped.

When Liam found them lying there a short while later, the glass fell from his nerveless hand and shattered to the floor at his feet. There was a ringing in his ears, the pounding of blood as his body fought to stay upright. He wanted to scream, to shout—to reject the truth of what lay clearly before him.

But there was his daughter to think of.

"C-come here, baby," he managed, even as tears began to fall. "Let's—let's leave Mammy to sleep."

CHAPTER 2

South London

One month later

Doctor Alexander Gregory seated himself in one of the easy chairs arranged around a low coffee table in his office, then nodded towards the security liaison nurse who hovered in the doorway.

"I'll take it from here, Pete."

The man glanced briefly at the other occupant in the room, then stepped outside to station himself within range, should his help be required.

After the door clicked shut, Gregory turned his attention to the woman seated opposite. Cathy Jones was in her early sixties but looked much younger; as though life's cares had taken very little toll. Her hair was dyed and cut into a snazzy style by a mobile hairdresser who visited the hospital every few weeks. She wore jeans and a cream wool jumper, but no jewellery—as per the rules. Her fingernails were painted a daring shade of purple and she had taken time with her make-up, which was flawless. For all the world, she could have been one of the smart, middle-aged women he saw sipping rosé at a wine bar in the city, dipping focaccia bread into small bowls of olive oil and balsamic while they chatted with their friends about the latest episode of *Strictly Come Dancing*.

That is, if she hadn't spent much of the past thirty years detained under the Mental Health Act.

"It's nice to see you again, Cathy. How was your week?"

They went through a similar dance every Thursday afternoon, where he asked a series of gentle, social questions to put her at ease, before attempting to delve into the deeper ones in accordance with her care plan. Though he was generally optimistic by nature, Gregory did not hold out any great hope that, after so long in the system, the most recent strategy of individual and group sessions, art and music therapy, would bring this woman any closer to re-entering normal society—but he had to try.

Cathy leaned forward suddenly, her eyes imploring him to listen.

"I wanted to speak to you, Doctor," she said, urgently. "It's about the next review meeting."

"Your care plan was reviewed recently," he said, in an even tone. "Don't you remember?"

There was a flicker of frustration, quickly masked.

"The clinical team made a mistake," she said.

"Oh? What might that be?"

Gregory crossed one leg lightly over the other and reached for his notepad, ready to jot down the latest theory she had cobbled together to explain the reason for her being there in the first place. In thirty years as a patient in four different secure hospitals, under the care of numerous healthcare professionals, Cathy had never accepted the diagnosis of her condition.

Consequently, she hadn't shown a scrap of remorse for her crimes, either.

"Well, I was reading only the other day about that poor, *poor* mother whose baby died. You know the one?"

Gregory did. The tragic case of Sudden Infant Death Syndrome had been widely reported in the press, but he had no intention of sating this woman's lust for tales of sensational child-deaths.

"Anyway, all those years ago, when they put me in *here*, the doctors didn't know so much about cot death. Not as much as they do now. If they had, things might have been different—"

Gregory looked up from his notepad, unwilling to entertain the fantasies that fed her illness.

"Do you remember the reason the pathologist gave for the deaths of your daughter, Emily, and your son, Christopher? Neither of them died following Sudden Infant Death Syndrome, as I think you're well aware."

The room fell silent, and she stared at him with mounting hatred, which he studiously ignored. Somewhere behind the reinforced glass window, they heard the distant buzz of a security gate opening.

"It was a cover up," she said, eventually. "You doctors are all the same. You always cover for each other. My children were *ill*, and not one of those quacks knew what to do about it—"

Gregory weighed up the usefulness of fishing out the pathology reports completed in 1987 following the murders of a two-year-old boy and a girl of nine months.

Not today.

"I'm going to appeal the court ruling," she declared, though every one of her previous attempts had failed. "You know what your problem is, Doctor? You've spent so long working with crackpots, you can't tell when a sane person comes along."

She'd tried this before, too. It was a favourite pastime of hers, to try to beat the doctor at his own game. It was a classic symptom of Munchausen syndrome by proxy that the sufferer developed an obsessive interest in the medical world, and its terminology. Usually, in order to find the best way to disguise the fact they were slowly, but surely, killing their own children.

"How did it make you feel, when your husband left you, Cathy?"

Gregory nipped any forthcoming tirade neatly in the bud, and she was momentarily disarmed. Then, she gave an ugly laugh.

"Back to that old chestnut again, are we?"

When he made no reply, she ran an agitated hand through her hair.

"How would any woman feel?" she burst out. "He left me with three children, for some *tart* with cotton wool for brains. I was well rid of him."

But her index finger began to tap against the side of the chair.

Tap, tap, tap.

Tap, tap, tap.

"When was the divorce finalised, Cathy?"

"It's all there in your bloody file, isn't it?" she spat. "Why bother to ask?"

"I'm interested to know if you remember."

"Sometime in 1985," she muttered. "January, February...Emily was only a couple of months old. The bastard was at it the whole time I was pregnant."

"That must have been very hard. Why don't you tell me about it?"

Her eyes skittered about the room, all of her previous composure having evaporated.

"There's nothing to tell. He buggered off to Geneva to live in a bloody great mansion with his Barbie doll, while I was left to bring up his children.

He barely even called when Emily was rushed into hospital. When *any* of them were."

"Do you think their...*illness*, would have improved, if he had?"

She gave him a sly look.

"How could it have made a difference? They were suffering from very rare conditions, outside our control."

Gregory's lips twisted, but he tried again.

"Did a part of you hope that news of their 'illness' might have encouraged your husband to return to the family home?"

"I never thought of it," she said. "All of my thoughts and prayers were spent trying to save my children."

He glanced up at the large, white plastic clock hanging on the wall above her head.

It was going to be a long morning.

An hour after Gregory finished his session with Cathy, he had just finished typing up his notes when a loud siren began to wail.

He threw open the door to his office and ran into the corridor, where the emergency alarm was louder still, echoing around the walls in a cacophony of sound. He took a quick glance in both directions and spotted a red flashing light above the doorway of one of the patients' rooms. He sprinted towards it, dimly aware of running footsteps following his own as others responded to whatever awaited them beyond the garish red light.

The heels of his shoes skidded against the floor as he reached the open doorway, where he found one of the ward nurses engaged in a mental battle with a patient who had fashioned a rudimentary knife from a sharpened fragment of metal and was presently holding it against her own neck.

Gregory reached for the alarm button and, a moment later, the wailing stopped. In the residual silence, he took a deep breath and fell back on his training.

"Do you mind if I come in?" he asked, holding out his hands, palms outstretched in the universal gesture for peace.

He exchanged a glance with the nurse, who was holding up well. He'd never ascribed to old-school hierarchies within hospital walls; doctors were no better equipped to deal with situations of this kind than an experienced mental health nurse—in fact, the reverse was often true. Life at Southmoor High Security Psychiatric Hospital followed a strict routine, for very good reason. Depending on their level of risk, patients were checked at least every fifteen minutes to try to prevent suicide attempts being made, even by those who had shown no inclination before, or who had previously been judged 'low risk'.

Especially those.

There were few certainties in the field of mental healthcare, but uncertainty was one of them.

"I'd like you to put the weapon down, Hannah," he said, calmly. "It's almost lunchtime, and it's Thursday. You know what that means."

As he'd hoped, she looked up, her grip on the knife loosening a fraction.

"Jam roly-poly day," he smiled. It was a mutual favourite of theirs and, in times of crisis, he needed to find common ground.

Anything to keep her alive.

"Sorry, Doc," she whispered, and plunged the knife into her throat.

It was a long walk back to his office, but when Gregory eventually returned some time later, he found he was not alone. A man of around fifty was seated at his desk, twirling idly on the chair while he thumbed through the most recent edition of *Psychology Today*. He wore a bobbled woollen jumper over a pair of ancient corduroy slacks, and brought with him the subtle odour of Murray Mints.

"Are you lost?"

The man looked up from the magazine and broke into a wide smile that was quickly extinguished when he spotted the bloodstains on Gregory's shirtsleeves. He rose from the desk chair and walked around to greet his protégé with open arms.

"Not all who wander are lost, m' boy."

Gregory was engulfed in a bear-like hug, which he returned, before stepping away to unbutton the shirt that clung to his skin and carried the faint, tinny odour of drying blood.

"What happened, Alex?"

"Suicide attempt by one of the regulars," he replied. "She came through."

He neglected to mention his own actions in keeping her alive…